He needed this far

Xav pulled Ash toward
"You still smell like peaches, you're still ~~~~
water and you still fit right under my heart."

"I am the hunted one," Ash said quietly. "You're trying
to protect me."

"Gage, Shaman, Kendall and Ashlyn," he said against
her hair, drinking in the scent of her and the feel of
her in his arms.

"What?"

"Those are the middle names I choose. And you
should be impressed with my ability to select baby
names when I didn't even know I was a father four
hours ago. Briar Kendall, Skye Ashlyn, Valor Shaman
and Thorn Gage. Phillips. Named after my brothers
and sister. Have to have the other side of the family
represented."

She moved out of his arms. "Callahan, not Phillips."

He hauled her into his lap as he sat down on the
poufy old-fashioned sofa. "Here's the deal. You
marry me, and you can pick all the names."

Dear Reader,

We always knew that Ashlyn and Xav were destined to be together—but who knows if the Callahan family can survive the evil from the past that has long haunted them?

Ash Callahan is a free spirit, and in her soul rests the future of Rancho Diablo. There's only one man who can help her find her family's happy ending—but her four darling babies are a secret Ash must keep for now!

Xav Phillips knows only one thing: he must find Ash and bring her home to the ranch where she belongs in time for Christmas. It's never easy to convince the silver-haired wild woman he has loved for so long about anything, but he knows his new—rather large—family is meant to live at Rancho Diablo. Convincing Ash to marry him and wear the magic wedding dress will be another challenge, yet as the past colors the future, Xav knows he must fight for a Callahan homecoming, the sweetest homecoming of all.

I hope you enjoy the final story in the Callahan legend. These were stories from my heart! The letters I've received about the Callahans let me know that this family touched your heart, too—thank you ever so much for your heartfelt support on this amazing journey!

Best wishes always,

Tina

www.TinaLeonard.com
www.Facebook.com/AuthorTinaLeonard
www.Facebook.com/TinaLeonardBooks
www.Twitter.com/Tina_Leonard

SWEET CALLAHAN HOMECOMING

—

TINA LEONARD

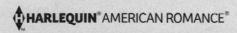
HARLEQUIN® AMERICAN ROMANCE®

Recycling programs
for this product may
not exist in your area.

ISBN-13: 978-0-373-75514-1

SWEET CALLAHAN HOMECOMING

Copyright © 2014 by Tina Leonard

ABOUT THE AUTHOR

Tina Leonard is a *USA TODAY* bestselling and award-winning author of more than fifty projects, including several popular miniseries for the Harlequin American Romance line. Known for bad-boy heroes and smart, adventurous heroines, her books have made the *USA TODAY*, Waldenbooks, Ingram and Nielsen BookScan bestseller lists. Born on a military base, Tina lived in many states before eventually marrying the boy who did her crayon printing for her in the first grade. You can visit her at www.tinaleonard.com, and follow her on Facebook and Twitter.

Books by Tina Leonard

HARLEQUIN AMERICAN ROMANCE

1129—MY BABY, MY BRIDE *
1137—THE CHRISTMAS TWINS *
1153—HER SECRET SONS *
1213—TEXAS LULLABY
1241—THE TEXAS RANGER'S TWINS
1246—THE SECRET AGENT'S SURPRISES‡
1250—THE TRIPLETS' RODEO MAN‡
1263—THE TEXAS TWINS
1282—THE COWBOY FROM CHRISTMAS PAST
1354—THE COWBOY'S TRIPLETSΩ
1362—THE COWBOY'S BONUS BABYΩ
1370—THE BULL RIDER'S TWINSΩ
1378—HOLIDAY IN A STETSON
        "A Rancho Diablo Christmas"
1385—HIS VALENTINE TRIPLETSΩ
1393—COWBOY SAM'S QUADRUPLETSΩ
1401—A CALLAHAN WEDDINGΩ
1411—THE RENEGADE COWBOY RETURNSΩ
1418—THE COWBOY SOLDIER'S SONSΩ
1427—CHRISTMAS IN TEXAS
        "Christmas Baby Blessings"
1433—A CALLAHAN OUTLAW'S TWINSΩ
1445—HIS CALLAHAN BRIDE'S BABYΩ
1457—BRANDED BY A CALLAHANΩ
1465—CALLAHAN COWBOY TRIPLETSΩ
1473—A CALLAHAN CHRISTMAS MIRACLEΩ
1481—HER CALLAHAN FAMILY MAN Ω

*The Tulips Saloon
‡The Morgan Men
ΩCallahan Cowboys

Grateful thanks to the many wonderful readers who walked with me on the journey to find the Callahan family's happy ending—I have been so blessed.

"The spirits guide us, and we heed the call."
—Chief Running Bear to his seven
Callahan warriors

Prologue

Ashlyn Callahan's six brothers stared at the man on the ground, then at their petite, silver-haired sister.

"Did you kill him, Ash?" Galen asked.

"Someone had to do it," Ash said, glaring at the semicircle of men whom she'd summoned to the stone-and-fire ring where evil Uncle Wolf had surprised her. As if she'd known that this was the moment she was born for, Ash had swiftly raised her weapon and fired. "You're the doctor, Galen. Check him out and see if it was a good hit."

Dante knelt near Wolf as Galen looked him over. Tighe stood close by her side, and Jace watched the canyons, keeping a wary eye out for Wolf's mercenaries. Falcon went to get Galen's medical bag from the military jeep, and Sloan headed up onto a nearby rock ledge to act as lookout. Her brothers supported her, and that support made her strong.

"If he's dead, know that I'm not sorry," Ash said flatly. She'd aimed to kill, and she was willing to admit it to anyone who asked, even though all the Callahans had been warned not to hurt their treacherous uncle. Their grandfather, Chief Running Bear, had always said that no harm was to befall his son Wolf—at least not from the family.

But because of Wolf and his cartel thugs, and their attempted takeover of Rancho Diablo, the Chacon Callahan parents, Julia and Carlos, had been in hiding for years. So had their Callahan cousins' parents, Jeremiah and Molly, who had built Rancho Diablo into the sprawling spread it was. The house—which was basically a castle as far as Ash was concerned—had seven chimneys and its Tudor style served as a beacon on the wide, panoramic landscape. But the ranch was more war zone than home ever since Wolf had decided to try to take it over. The Callahan children and grandchildren had never experienced what it was like to grow up here, as they were now in satellite safe locations, most of them in Hell's Colony, Texas, at the Phillips' compound.

It makes my blood boil. I suppose I snapped—but after Wolf tried to steal the black Diablos, after he incarcerated them in caves under the canyons, under our very ranch, and after he very nearly killed Jace, someone had to pull the trigger.

I'm always happy to pull the trigger, and this time it was especially rewarding.

Galen glanced up at her. "He's not dead," he said. "His pulse is very weak. With care, he can be saved."

Ash shrugged. "If you turn your backs, I'll roll him into the canyon for the vultures. If you save him to strike at us another day, I wash my hands of it."

Her brothers stared at her, and Tighe pulled her into his arms for a brotherly, comforting hug.

"It's okay, little sister," he murmured. "You don't always have to be the strong one."

They were all strong. No family was stronger than

hers. And although she carried her grandfather's spirit, it warred with the part of her soul that bowed to no one.

The lightning strike tattoo on her shoulder burned. All of them had the same tattoo—only hers had a minuscule star beside it, setting her apart.

I always knew I was the hunted one that Grandfather foretold, the one destined to bring darkness and devastation to Rancho Diablo. I always knew it was me, and I was never afraid.

She watched dispassionately as Galen and her brothers loaded their uncle into the jeep to take him to the hospital.

"I'll find my way back," Ash said. "You, my brothers, can play ambulance driver."

Sloan jumped down from the ledge and got in the vehicle. "Nice shooting, by the way. Wolf won't be too happy when he regains consciousness. See you soon, sis."

They drove away. She waited until they were long gone. Then Ash turned in the opposite direction, and with the stealth and speed she'd learned from Running Bear, she left the stone-and-fire ring—the place their grandfather had named as their home base while they fought for Rancho Diablo—and began the long journey away from her beloved family.

Chapter One

Nine months later

Xav Phillips had looked long and hard for Ash Callahan, and now, if his luck held, he might have finally caught up to her in a small town in Texas—Wild, Texas, to be precise. She'd done a good job of covering her tracks, but he'd learned a lot of beneficial things in the years he'd worked for the Callahans, and one of them was how to find something or somebody that didn't want to be found.

He wasn't sure what Ash saw in this bucolic place in the Hill Country in the heart of Texas, but he'd be willing to bet the serenity of the place had called to her.

Ashlyn Callahan had been in need of peace for many years.

He knocked on the door of the small, two-story white house perched on a grassy stretch of farmland. He noted the Christmas decorations twining the white posts on the porch and the twinkling tree situated in the window. Back at Rancho Diablo in New Mexico, Christmas would be in full swing. Aunt Fiona Callahan typically planned an annual Christmas ball—this year the ball had a fairy-tale theme—but she was missing the last

Callahan to be raffled at one of her shindigs. Ash had left the ranch and the town of Diablo after she'd allegedly shot her uncle Wolf Chacon. Fiona had begged Xav to find her niece, not just because she wanted her to be the final Callahan raffle "victim" at the ball, but because it was the holidays. It was time for Ash to come home, Fiona proclaimed, adding, "I'm not getting any younger! I want my family around."

So that was the excuse that sent him searching for Ash, but it wasn't the real reason he had to find her. Truth be told, he missed her like hell—a fact he wouldn't have admitted to a soul. Her six brawny brothers had no idea of the depth of his feelings for Ash, and there was no reason to share that with his employers.

And there were other urgent motives to find his platinum-haired girl. Most important, Ash didn't know that she had not been the one to shoot her uncle Wolf. She'd certainly tried. But in the melee of her uncle's appearance and Xav firing, Ash had never noticed that her weapon didn't recoil.

If her gun had been loaded, he was certain Wolf wouldn't have gotten off with only a punctured lung. Ash was a crack shooter.

But Ash's gun wasn't the one that fired the shot.

It had been his.

He'd unloaded Ash's gun that afternoon while she'd napped—after they'd made love. He'd unloaded it because they were alone in the canyons, and he'd been about to propose.

One didn't propose to Ash without taking proper precautions.

A man didn't love a woman as long as he'd loved Ash and lay his heart on the line without being fairly sure of himself. But one never knew what Ash would say or do—and so he had to be prepared for a refusal.

He'd planned his seduction carefully. Make love, disarm her, then proffer the best argument he had for hitting up the closest altar.

He'd even had a diamond-and-sapphire ring in his pocket to mark the occasion, if she was inclined to accept his offer of a partnership between them. A joining of the Callahan and Phillips families at long last. A merger between them, a professional alliance—the smoothest lasso he could design to draw Ash over to his side without her kicking and screaming. Ash was a practical woman; since a great many of the Callahan families were living at the Hell's Colony compound in Texas that he and his three siblings, Kendall, Gage and Shaman owned, it made sense to go easy on the emotions and heavy on practical.

But he'd never gotten to the proposal. Wolf had ambushed them, and Ash had shot him—or she thought she had. Xav had fired, too, and in the silence that fell as Wolf crumpled to the ground, Xav had taken her gun, fully intending to leave behind no trace of her involvement. There was no reason for her to be blamed.

Ash had sent him away, telling him this was a family matter, a fact with which he couldn't argue. She was stone-cold in her demand, and he'd departed, fully cognizant that Ash was calling her family to clean up, and no doubt for advice. As an employee of Rancho Diablo, Xav knew very well how the Callahans worked. They'd get there in a flash, and little sister would be up to her delicate shell-shaped ears in backup and support. The Callahans wouldn't let anything happen to Ash—and so he went off to ponder what he'd done over a beer.

He'd been stunned that he'd killed the uncle of the woman to whom he'd been about to propose. On the other hand, better he do it than Ash. As he knew too well, Chief Running Bear had forbidden his family to harm his son Wolf. Doing so would bring the family curse on them.

He'd wanted badly to protect Ash from that.

He'd fired so fast he wasn't sure Ash knew that he had.

But when the dust settled in the ensuing weeks, he'd waited for Ash to seek him out, as she had many times over the years. When she hadn't come, he'd gone looking for her at Rancho Diablo.

To his chagrin, he'd learned that his wild-at-heart angel hadn't been seen since that fateful day. And it turned out Galen's medical expertise had brought Wolf back from the brink. The old scoundrel had recovered and had slowly returned to taunting the Callahans. Yet Ash hadn't been seen or heard from by her family again—except last month when she'd sent a text to her family to wish them happy holidays.

It was that holiday message that had nearly broken Fiona. Fiona had summoned him, sending him off to find her beloved niece.

He'd accepted the mission gladly, knowing it wasn't going to be a cakewalk. Ash wasn't easy to track. She used only cash. There were no phone calls, no computer emails to track. It was as if she'd disappeared—which she'd obviously intended to do.

In the end, he'd gone to Running Bear for direction, only to be amazed that Running Bear hadn't heard from Ash, either. Those two shared the same untamed spirit.

But Xav got a pointer or two from Running Bear that

sent him on a path to find her. Now he shifted on the white-painted porch, hearing footsteps inside, hoping his journey wasn't a dead end. It had been too many months since he'd held the love of his life in his arms.

A middle-aged woman opened the door, a questioning frown on her face. "Yes?"

"Hi." He gave her his most friendly smile. "I'm Xav Phillips, from Diablo, New Mexico. I'm looking for a woman named Ashlyn Callahan."

The woman shook her head, glancing over her shoulder when a baby's cry burst in the background. "I'm sorry, no. I've never heard of her."

He couldn't say what made him linger on the porch. Maybe it was because he'd come so far and was so disappointed to find his search turning up a dead end again. Another baby's cries joined the first, sending up a wail of epic proportions between them, which made the woman anxiously begin to back away.

"Excuse me," she said, "good luck finding whomever you're looking for."

She closed the door. Xav hesitated, then leaned his ear against the wood. He heard soft voices inside comforting the babies, and then unbelievably, he heard a voice he'd know any day, any night, whether he was awake, asleep or even in a coma.

"Sweet baby, don't fuss. My little prince," he heard Ash say, and in a flash, he slid over to the enormous glass window framing the Christmas tree so he could peer cautiously inside the house.

Behind the large, ruffle-branched Christmas tree, four white bassinets lay together in a room decorated for the holidays amid beautifully wrapped gifts. He held his breath, watching Ash comfort a tiny infant boy. Ash's shock of pale hair had grown into a waterfall of silver liquid she wore in a ponytail. Xav grew warm all over despite the cold, and Cupid's arrow shot right into his heart, the same way it had every time he'd ever gotten within two miles of her.

He was head over heels in love with her, and nine long months apart had done nothing to diminish those emotions. The ring in his pocket practically burned, reminding him how long he'd waited to ask her to marry him.

She put the baby down and picked up another, a sweet, pink-pajamaed little girl, and Xav's heart felt like it splatted on the ground. She acted as if these were her children, so loving and gentle was she as she held them. Xav was poleaxed with new thoughts of making Ash a mother. Motherhood and Ash weren't a combination he'd ever really put together in his head, but watching her with these children made him realize his original proposal wasn't the one he wanted to offer her.

He didn't want to fall back on a business arrangement to save his ego.

No, he was going all in. He was going to tell her the truth about the shot she'd allegedly fired at Wolf, because clearly that was why she was hiding out here, helping the older lady babysit her family's babies. Or maybe she ran a babysitting service. It didn't matter. The point was, Ash was in hiding and he was going to tell her the truth: she was not the hunted one. She was not destined to bring destruction to Rancho Diablo and her family.

And then he was going to ask her to be his wife. His real true wife, to have and to hold, in sickness and health, in good times and better times, forever.

Xav hadn't realized he'd moved away from the protection of the twinkling Christmas tree in order to spy better, but Ash's suddenly astonished eyes jolted him out of his reverie. She stared at him over the pink blanket-wrapped baby, her lips parted with shock to see him standing among the evergreen bushes at the window. And then, to his complete dismay, Ash snapped the curtains closed.

A screeching siren split the air. Someone had hit some kind of panic button inside the house, which meant police would be on the way. He was certain Ash had recognized him, but just to be certain she didn't think he was an intruder, he leaped up on the porch and pushed the door open.

"Hi, beautiful," Xav said, and she looked at him, completely speechless, and suddenly pain crashed through him. The last thing Xav remembered thinking was how lucky it was that he'd finally located the most footloose Callahan of them all.

He'd succeeded on Fiona's mission.

Callahan bonus points for sure.

"WHAT DO WE DO WITH HIM?" Mallory McGrath asked, and Ash tried to force her flabbergasted mind to think rationally. It wasn't easy, and not just because Mallory had set off the panic button on the security system, which was wailing like mad. She crossed to the system pad and shut the silly thing off before staring down at the lean cowboy sprawled on the floor. How many hours had she spent thinking about Xav Phillips over the past few months, especially during her pregnancy? How many times had she wanted to call him to come to her, yet knowing she couldn't place him in that kind of danger? Anyone from Rancho Diablo who had any contact with her would be in jeopardy—the Callahans had learned that the hard way, time and again, over the many years they'd battled Uncle Wolf and the cartel. It was no game they were playing, but a full-fledged fight for survival.

Sometimes it felt as though they were losing. It almost always seemed as if they might not ever defeat an enemy that was determined to destroy the ranch and the Callahan legacy. Good didn't always conquer evil.

Ash knelt down to move Xav's long, ebony hair out of his face. "Poor Xav. I could have told you that you should stay away from me." The tree twinkled, sending soft colorful light against his drawn skin. "What am I going to do with you now?" she asked him, though she knew she wouldn't get an answer.

She was startled when he opened his eyes. "Marry me," Xav said. "You can marry me, damn it, and tell the woman with the wrought-iron Santa Claus she whaled upside my noggin that I come in peace."

"Xav!" She wanted to kiss him so badly, yet didn't dare. Of course his marriage proposal wasn't sincere; clearly a concussion rendered him temporarily senseless. "Can you sit up? Mallory, will you get him a glass of water?"

"Who is he?" Mallory asked, reluctantly setting down her festive weapon.

"Just a family friend," Ash said, her gaze on Xav as his eyes locked on hers.

"*Friend* my ass," Xav growled. "Do you have any idea how hard it was to find you? Do friends search every nook and cranny of Texas and parts in between to find each other?"

"Definitely a concussion," Ash said, frowning at the

big handsome man, all long body and sinewy muscles. "I've never heard him talk like that."

"Hello, I'm right here," Xav said crustily, trying to rise.

Ash pushed him back to the floor. "Take a minute to gather your wits, cowboy."

"My wits have never been so gathered." He sat up and glared at her, then stared at his brown cowboy hat mournfully. "She killed it."

Mallory had the nerve to giggle, and Xav looked even more disgusted, as if he thought it rude that someone laughed at crushing his cowboy hat with a Santa Claus doorstop before they'd been introduced.

"It'll be all right." Ash took the hat from him, put it on a chair, inspected his head. "I do believe that hat saved your thick skull. There's not a scratch on you."

"Well, thanks for that." He stood, and Ash steered him toward one of Mallory's soft, old-fashioned Victorian sofas. Before she could get him past the babies and onto the sofa, Xav stopped, staring down into the bassinettes, transfixed by the tiny infants inside. The four babies slept peacefully, undisturbed by the strong, determined male visitor in their midst.

"Hmm," Xav said, "pretty cute little stinkweeds."

For all the times she'd envisioned introducing the babies to their father, never had she imagined he'd call his adorable offspring stinkweeds. Ash stiffened, her bubble bursting, and Mallory laughed and excused herself, saying she was going to go hunt up some tea and cinnamon cake.

"Stinkweeds?" Ash demanded. "Is that the best you can do?"

Xav hunkered down on the sofa, rubbed his head.

"I think at the moment, yes. In a minute, when the headache passes, I can probably be more creative." He looked at her. "You didn't introduce me to your friend, but I assume these babies are her grandkids?"

He must have noted her astonished expression because he quickly said, "Or are you running a babysitting service?"

Great. He might seem fine after a crack on the head, but the truth was going to blow his mind.

On the other hand, maybe it was best if Xav didn't know he was a father. She could convince him to go on his merry way and never look back.

No. That didn't sound right, either. He'd tracked her down, he was here. These were his children. There was no going back.

"Actually, Xav," she said, "these aren't Mallory's babies."

"Ah, well. It's not important." He reached into a bassinet and touched one baby gently. "If I'd drawn them in a poker game, I'd say they were a perfect four of a kind."

Her heart melted just a bit, dislodged from its frozen perch. "Really? You think they're perfect?"

"Sure. I've seen tons of rugrats around Rancho Diablo. These are cute. Look a bit like tiny elves with scrunched red faces." He stood, picked his hat up off the sofa where Mallory had put it, stared at the damaged crown with a raised brow. "But I didn't come here to admire someone's kids, Ash." He looked into her eyes, and her heart responded with a dangerous flutter. "I've come to take you home for the holidays."

Chapter Two

"That's not possible, Xav," Ash told him, her gaze sincere.

He hated it when someone told him something wasn't possible. It reminded him of his father, Gil Phillips, of Gil Phillips, Inc., who'd run the business and the Hell's Colony compound with an iron fist. Gil had never let anybody tell him something was impossible, and the only person on earth who'd ever been able to talk Gil off his high horse was their mother. In business, Gil wouldn't have tolerated an employee who thought anything was impossible.

Xav was pretty certain he'd developed his father's stubbornness, especially where Ash was concerned. He drank her in, wished he could sneak a kiss.

And a lot more.

"Everything's possible, little darling. You wouldn't deny your aunt Fiona the pleasure of having all her nephews and her niece home at Christmas, would you?"

"It's not possible," Ash said again with a shake of that platinum hair he loved so much, the ponytail swinging with her negative vibe.

Wasn't she just too cute? She had no idea that he was a man who didn't believe in impossible.

"I'll give you five minutes to pack up," he said, his

tone kind and convincing, the tone he'd used many times in his father's boardroom—before Xav had gone to live the Callahan way.

Life as a corporate suit was very far in his past. He had a few rougher edges now.

"Five minutes to pack," he reiterated, "and if you're not standing by my truck ready to hit the road, I'm tossing you over my shoulder and carrying you out of here, caveman-style. And don't think I won't do it, beautiful. I'm not going to be the man who disappoints Fiona at Christmas, not when she sent me on this quest to bring you home. It's her heart's desire." He smiled at Ash. "It's an assignment I have no intention of failing."

"Well, you'll have to." Ash turned away from him. "I can't go back."

How well he knew this woman—he could practically read her mind. He knew the curve of her neck, and the way she crossed her arms denoting Callahan intractability. Xav walked up behind her, put his arms around her, comforting and close—but not too close.

Not as close as he wanted to be—not nearly close enough.

"I know you're afraid," he murmured, and Ash went straight as a board in his arms. "Bad word choice," he backtracked. "I know you think you killed Wolf, Ash. You didn't."

She turned to face him. "I tried to kill him. If I didn't, it doesn't matter. I meant to. I'd shoot him again the first chance I got."

He wanted to kiss her so badly. Maybe she sensed it, because she stepped out of his arms, away from him. Put three feet between them.

"I can never go home," Ash said. "I'm staying here."

She looked at the sleeping babies with a sweet smile, then looked up at him. "How are my brothers? And Aunt Fiona? Uncle Burke? Grandfather Running Bear?"

He'd made love to this woman so many times that he practically knew her every thought, and right now, he knew she was avoiding his mission, dismissing it, as Ash dismissed everything that didn't square with her worldview. Ash had always been fiercely independent, despite her six doting older brothers, and in a strange way, they depended on their sister more than she depended upon them.

Ash was the spirit of the Callahan clan.

She had to learn that she didn't have to carry the weight of the world on her delicate shoulders forever.

And anyway, a man was only as good as his promises.

He picked her up, tossed her over one shoulder and marched her to the front door.

"Put me down!"

He spanked her bottom once lightly with a satisfying *smack!* against her jeans, drawing another outraged protest. She pinched him smartly under his arm, hard enough to force a grunt from him.

"Put me down!" she commanded again, as if he would have listened when he finally had her in his arms.

Two squad cars pulled in front of the house, and the next thing he knew, a couple of Wild's finest were yelling at him to put the little lady down.

"I forgot to call and tell the sheriff it was a false alarm," Ash said, apologetic, as he set her gently on the ground. She was breathless and a bit tousled from being upside down. "You'd better go."

"I'm not going anywhere until you agree to go with

me." He could be just as stubborn as she. "Go tell the sheriff and his friends that their services aren't needed."

"It would be better if you go."

She gazed up at him, and he caught a funny bit of desperation from her. "Nope," he said, still wearing stubborn like a badge.

"Ash, is there a problem?" the sheriff asked, and Ash looked at Xav.

"*Is* there a problem?" she asked Xav, and he realized she was holding him hostage to her demand that he leave.

Well, he'd never been one to go down without a fight.

"Hell, yeah, there's a problem, Sheriff. This woman won't accept my marriage proposal. I drove all the way from Rancho Diablo in New Mexico to propose to her. Xav Phillips," he said, shaking the sheriff's hand.

The sheriff and his deputies snickered a little at his conundrum. Then the sheriff perked up. "Xav Phillips, Gil Phillips's son, from Hell's Colony?"

"Yes, sir," Xav said politely.

"I knew your daddy before you were even a twinkle in his eye," the sheriff said, drawing a groan from Ash. The sheriff turned to her.

"Ashlyn Callahan, you hit the panic button because some man has proposed to you? Again?" The sheriff shook his head. "He drives a nice truck, comes from a great family, practically Texas royalty. If Santa brings you a father for those four children of yours, you might treat him a little nicer than calling the law on him." He tipped his hat to Ash, shook Xav's hand again, and he and his deputies got back in their squad cars. "Good luck," the sheriff said to Xav through his open window.

"Probably five men in the county have offered to marry this lady, and she's turned them all down flat."

He nodded. "Forewarned, Sheriff. Thanks."

"Are all of you through enjoying a manly guffaw at my expense?" Ash demanded. "Because if you are, I need to get back in the house. I have children who need me."

"Good night, Sheriff." He followed Ash back inside, his mind niggling with discomfort and alarm. Five men had proposed to her? Ash picked up a baby that was sending up a gentle wail and sat down on the old-fashioned sofa situated across from the Christmas tree.

He sat next to her. "Hey, Ash," he said, "the sheriff said something about you needing a father for your children, that Santa had sent you one for Christmas. It was a figure of speech, right?" He looked at her, surprised but not displeased in the slightest that she was undoing the pearl buttons on her white sweater. She tossed a baby blanket over her shoulder, obscuring the baby's face—and suddenly, it hit Xav like a thunderclap that Ash was *nursing* that baby.

Which would not be the slightest bit possible unless these were her children. He stared at Ash, and she looked back at him calmly, her denim-blue eyes unworried and clear.

"You're a *mother*," he said, feeling light-headed, and not from the crack Mallory had landed on his skull. "These are your babies?"

She nodded, and he got dizzy. The woman he loved was a mother, and somehow she'd had four children. This perfect four of a kind was hers.

It wasn't possible. But he could hear gentle sucking sounds occasionally, and he knew it was as possible as the sun coming up the next day. He felt weak all over, weak-kneed in a way he'd never been, his heart splintering like shattered glass.

"Damn, Ash, your family…you haven't told them."

"No, I haven't."

A horrible realization sank into him, painful and searing. "Who's the father?"

She frowned. "A dumb ornery cowboy."

"That doesn't sound like you. You wouldn't fall for a dumb ornery cowboy."

"Yes, I would," Ash said. "I would, and I did."

He looked at the tiny bundles of sweetness in their bassinets. Two girls, a boy, and he presumed that was a boy underneath the blanket at his mother's breast, because each bassinet had colored blankets, two pink, two blue. Two of each. He felt sad, sick, really, that the woman he adored had found someone else in the nine months she'd been gone. He felt a little betrayed, sure that the two of them had shared something, although neither of them had ever tried to quantify exactly what it was they'd shared. "He really is dumb if he's not here taking care of you," Xav said, and it had to be the truth or she wouldn't be living with the woman with the wicked swing who'd tried to crush his cranium. "Ash, I'll marry you, and take care of you, and your children," he said suddenly, realizing how he could finally catch the woman of his dreams without even appearing to be the love-struck schmuck that he was.

If anyone was father material, it was he.

"YOU'LL MARRY ME?" Ash repeated, outraged. "You'll marry me, you big, dumb, ornery—"

He held up a hand. "Of course I will. I'd do anything for a friend, and I consider you one of my dearest friends. A sister. I'll give your children my name, and I'll protect you, Ash."

If she hadn't been nursing Thorn, she'd have given the gorgeous sexy hunk next to her another knock on the head to match the lump he probably already sported. "I don't want to get married. And I certainly wouldn't marry you."

"You have to get married, Ash." She heard the concern in his voice. "Your brothers are going to have a fit when they find out you're a single mother and the father won't step up. They'll drag him to the altar for sure. And it won't be pretty. Your brothers can be tough when crossed, you know that."

Mallory bustled in with some cake and tea on a wicker tray. She handed Xav a cup and looked at him directly. "So, when's the wedding?"

"Mallory," Ash said, and Xav said, "As soon as I can convince Ash that getting married is the right thing to do."

"I should think so," Mallory said as she leaned over to pick up one of the girls. "After all, I would have thought you'd have been here for the birth. Ash said you'd never find her, but I had a feeling you would. A man belongs with his family."

Xav's gaze landed on her. She glared at Mallory, wishing her friend would cease with the barrage of information. "Mallory, Xav and I haven't really had a chance to talk things out."

"Oh, pooh," Mallory told the baby she'd picked up. "If we wait on your mother to talk things out, you'll never have a father. Xav, meet your daughter Skye." She handed him the baby, which he took, and not as gingerly as Ash might have wanted. "And this is Valor," Mallory continued, pointing to the last baby in his white bassinet, "and that little fellow being held by his mother is Thorn. This little angel is Briar. Children, meet your father. Please help yourself to the cake, Xav. You'd better eat while you can. Once these little babies get tuned up, they tend to want everything at once. It's quite the diaper rodeo."

Mallory left the room, pleased with herself. Ash could barely meet Xav's eyes, but she made herself look at him.

He looked the way she'd known he would—thunderstruck. Astonished. Maybe even a little angry.

"*I'm* the big, dumb, ornery cowboy?"

She nodded. "I'm sorry. I shouldn't have phrased it quite that way." The moment had come upon her so unexpectedly that she hadn't handled any of it well. "I wish I'd found a different way to tell you, Xav."

"These are my babies?" He sounded absolutely incredulous, rocked. Dumbfounded.

She nodded, words seeming inadequate.

He hesitated, stared at the baby in his arms. "I don't understand. You've been gone a long time. When did this happen? When were you going to tell me?"

So many questions, so few answers. He wasn't going to be happy with any answer she gave him, and she couldn't blame him. "The night I shot Uncle Wolf," she began, faltering a little at the expression in his eyes. He still looked angry. "The night I shot Wolf, I was going to tell you I'd just learned I was pregnant," she rushed out.

The baby in his arms began a snuffling sort of wail, which startled the baby she was nursing. Which got the other two going, and suddenly there was no time to explain more.

An hour later, they collapsed on the sofa, worn out, all babies fed, changed and asleep in their bassinets.

"They're down for twenty minutes," Ash said. "You should probably go, while you still can."

He looked at her. "We've got a thousand things to talk about, and a lot you have to tell me. But you can't stay here. You can't keep these babies from their family, from Rancho Diablo. You can't keep them from Fiona." He looked so serious, so very serious, that the automatic *no* died on her lips. "Can you imagine how her Christmas would explode with joy—times four? You can't cheat her of Christmas with her whole family, not to mention you can't deny your grandfather, Running Bear, knowing the next generation of his great-grandchildren." He reached out to touch her hand. "These babies will never know their grandparents, Ash. You can't keep them from their great-grandfather. The chief's one of the finest men I've ever known."

Tears jumped into her eyes. "Grandfather is one of the finest men to ever walk the planet," Ash said. "Thank you for respecting him."

"Respect him, hell. I want to be him."

She smiled. "We all do."

"Anyway," Xav said, "in these babies flows Callahan blood. You've got to take them home, tell your family the truth of why you left."

"I didn't leave because I was pregnant. I left because I knew I'd brought trouble to Rancho Diablo and my family when I disobeyed Grandfather by killing Wolf. You don't understand what it's like to bring a curse upon your own family."

"No, but I do understand you have a bigger problem, beautiful, which is what your brothers are going to do to you when they find out you had four little Callahans and kept them out of the whole process. You shared in all their pregnancies, the joy, the misery, all of it." He shook his head.

"You're not telling me anything I don't know. I didn't make the decision to leave lightly. You were there, you know I went against Grandfather's teachings."

He shrugged. "Your brothers are still going to be hot with you about this. Not as hot as I am, but they're going to be awfully let down."

"I couldn't tell you," Ash said. "You'd have followed me anywhere I went if you'd known I was pregnant."

"I followed you anyway. Babies didn't figure into my equation, but I wasn't about to let the trail go cold." He looked at her and shook his head again. "You little devil. When were you going to tell me?"

That was the question she had asked herself many times: When should she tell Xav he was a father?

There had been no good answers. If she'd told him where she was, she'd have to tell all the family—hardly a way to keep them safe. "Xav, you don't understand. I know you think you're a Callahan now, but you're not. You didn't grow up understanding that some things just can't be explained. Spiritual and mystical things."

"The ghosts at Rancho Diablo aren't any worse than the ones at the Phillips compound, I assure you."

She shook her head impatiently. "I don't mean secrets, I'm talking about spirits. We live our lives by the spirits. And there are evil spirits in the world. One of them is Uncle Wolf. I wasn't about to bring tragedy on my children by exposing them to him."

"It makes sense, but it also sounds like you don't think I can protect you or my own flesh and blood. I assure you I can, and I will."

It was so true what Xav said. Somehow she'd known he'd find her eventually. Their paths were meant to cross again.

She'd just thought it would be further in the future. Past the holidays, away from sentiment and the longing for home at Christmas that had come over her lately. "Like Mallory said, this is Briar," she said, pointing to her firstborn, "and her sister is Skye. Skye's my special one." She reached a gentle finger to stroke Skye's back. The baby slept on, undisturbed. "Skye is a Down's syndrome baby, and my happiest spirit. She rarely fusses, just really wants to snuggle. Skye has Grandfather Running Bear's spirit. It's strong in her. Briar is strong physically. She always keeps her head turned toward her sister. I think she's determined to protect her." She looked at Xav. He was smiling, his eyes peaceful as he listened, so she continued. "This is Thorn. He was born second, and had some lung issues for a while. But the doctors expect him to make a full recovery. And this is Valor," she said, gently patting her last son. "It was touch and go for him for a while, and I really thought I might lose him. All of them were underweight, of course, so there was a lot of time in the hospital. They've only been home with me for about three weeks. Valor became stronger and stronger, and now I really believe he's going to be a warrior like Running Bear. I can feel him listening to the world around him, and I know he's taking it all in."

"When were they born?"

"October 15. Cesarean section. Briar came home

first, then Valor. Thorn and Skye came home together the day before Thanksgiving, so I felt very blessed. Mallory's been a rock. I couldn't have done it without her."

Xav got up, stalked to the window. "I wish I'd been here. I *should* have been here."

"I wish things could have been different. But everything changed when I shot my uncle. It set things in motion I had no control over. And since you've spent the last several years working at Rancho Diablo, you know that as well as anyone."

Chapter Three

Briar, Thorn, Skye and Valor—all strong names. Xav looked at his children with amazement and some lingering shock. How had this happened? How had he become a father of four, as easily as if a Fiona-style fairy godmother had waved her magic wand at him, gifting him with a full-blown family?

God, he couldn't blame this on Fiona or even a fairy godmother, even though Fiona had totally and not too subtly plotted to enlarge her Callahan family tree. All the Callahans, every last one of them, had fallen to Fiona's legendary and epic lures and chicanery to see her family with families of their own, but Ash won the prize for secret babypalooza. He stared in shock at his four offspring, trying to figure out how his world had changed when he wasn't paying attention.

The "magic" had simply been an old-fashioned condom malfunction and his own raging desire to have the blonde sylph currently sitting on the sofa every which way from Sunday any chance he could reel her in.

She'd not been as reelable as he would have liked, and consequently, he'd spent most of his years with a serious case of unrequited longing. And every time he'd thought he'd had Ash, she'd disappeared again, leaving him satisfied for the moment but drained emotionally because who knew how long he'd have to wait until the next time she showed up in the canyons wearing a smile that made him virtually her love captive?

Undaunted, he'd played a waiting game, slightly uncomfortable because he felt guilty luring the sister of the men whom he considered good friends and employers. So he had to wait for Ash to come to him to lessen his guilt, when he really wanted to ride off with her into the canyons and drown himself in her for days.

"I left the middle names for you," Ash said, snapping him out of his tangled thoughts. "I thought you'd want to have some say in naming your children."

So Ash *had* eventually planned to tell him. He felt a little better. "How did four happen?"

She shrugged. "I wanted them, and they wanted me."

What kind of an answer was that? Coming from Ash, it was almost reasonable, but he needed more grounding. "I'm not sure I understand."

"I asked the spirits for a big family. I always wanted four children. I didn't realize I'd get them all at once, but I feel really blessed." She smiled, and she was the most beautiful woman in the world to his Ashlyn-starved eyes. "These babies agreed to be my family."

The answer somehow made absolute sense to him. Whatever Ash wanted, Ash believed she would get— and so her wishes usually happened exactly the way she dreamed them. It was her force of spirit and confidence that commanded the earth and stars around her.

Except for Wolf, who she had no command over, and the reason she was here.

"Look, Ash, I know why you went away. I know you think you're the hunted one your grandfather always warned about. But I shot Wolf. So you're not the hunted one." It was so important that she understand this, because they needed to put their family together.

He needed this family. He needed *her*.

Xav pulled her toward him, wrapped her in his arms. She seemed so surprised she didn't fight him, so he took advantage of her momentary lull in willpower and enjoyed the moment. Memories washed over him. "You still smell like peaches, you're still soft as rainwater and you still fit right under my heart."

"I *am* the hunted one," Ash said quietly. "You're trying to protect me."

"Gage, Shaman, Kendall and Ashlyn," he said against her hair, drinking in the scent of her and the feel of her in his arms.

"What?"

"Those are the middle names I choose. And you should be impressed with my ability to select names when I didn't even know I was a father four hours ago. Briar Kendall, Skye Ashlyn, Valor Shaman and Thorn Gage. Phillips. Named after my brothers and sister. Have to have the other side of the family represented."

She moved out of his arms, and he decided not to try to pull her back. "Callahan, not Phillips."

He hauled her into his lap as he sat down on the poufy old-fashioned sofa. "Here's the deal. You marry me and you can pick all the names."

"No," Ash said, "I like the names you chose."

"Great. Now," he said, taking the diamond-and-sapphire ring from his pocket, "here's what I was going to give you the last night we were together. Put it on your delicate little finger and tell me when and where we're going to gather for a wedding."

She stared at the ring. "Were you really going to give that to me before Wolf ambushed us?"

He nodded. "It was a very disappointing interruption, I'll admit." Nine months of an interruption. "I would have proposed at some appropriate point after I shot Wolf, but you disappeared. Which I would appreciate you not doing again." He looked at his children. "I want to give these children my name as soon as possible."

She handed him back the ring. "As beautiful as this ring is, I can't marry you."

"I can't make love to you until you do."

Ash cocked a brow. "Who says I want you to make love to me?"

He kissed her, taking his time, before she finally pushed him gently away. "You want me to make love to you right now, Ashlyn Callahan."

Ash got out of his lap. "Xav, you don't understand."

"I understand that we belong together. That's all I need to know. The only reason you're saying no is because you don't believe that I shot Wolf. Let me tell you how that went down," Xav said. "I had unloaded your gun."

"No one gets my gun away from me." She looked at the babies with a fond smile. "Of course, that was before I became a mother. Now I never carry."

"I made love to you, and while you dozed, I took the precaution of removing the bullets from your gun."

"Why?" She shot him a suspicious look.

"Because, my sweet peach, you have your unpredictable moments, and I was about to propose." He waved the ring box at her. "I figured my chances were fifty-fifty that you might say yes. Or you might decide to tell me to walk the plank." He grinned, pleased with himself. "I'm a cautious man."

"You thought I'd shoot you over a marriage proposal?"

"It was just a precaution. I like putting odds in my favor. I've learned a lot from the Callahans over the years."

She sighed. "Xav, I appreciate you trying to lift the burden of guilt from me, but your story makes no sense whatsoever. I'd know if a gun I fired didn't have a round in it. But you're a hero for trying to make me think I'm not the hunted one. I know I am."

She drifted out of the room, his gaze longingly on the petite body he remembered so well. Missed so much. When she was gone, he looked at his four children. "If you four got even a teaspoon of your mother's obstinate streak, you'll be able to survive anything the world throws at you."

Mallory came in, set a tray in front of him. "Green chili? Tea?"

His stomach rumbled a bit since he hadn't touched the cake she'd brought in before. "Both. Thanks."

Mallory sat across from him, busied herself with the tray. "I've heard a lot about you."

"All good, I hope."

"You definitely live up to Ash's description."

"Which was what?"

"Tall, dark, handsome."

Mallory had a wealth of freckles, sparkling eyes, and dark hair pulled back in a neat ponytail. She radiated good humor. "Thanks for helping out with my crew."

"Ash also mentioned you weren't the settling-down type," Mallory continued.

"I just proposed," Xav said. "Although the lady hasn't accepted yet. She's thinking it over."

Mallory smiled. "Ash said she chased you for years, but that you weren't a man who could be caught."

He wondered why Ash would tell her friend such a story. "My proposal even came with a ring."

"I believe you," Mallory said. "I'm just giving you a little tip. I'm off to bake cupcakes before the babies wake up. They don't sleep long during the day. Or the night. It's nice to meet you, Xav. Feel free to stay in our home if Ash invites you."

She left, and Xav considered his options. Of course he was staying here with his children!

Actually, Ash hadn't invited him. He might not be invited. Even offering an engagement ring, a guy might find himself sleeping in his truck. And what was that business about him not being a man who could be caught?

It was Ash Callahan who'd run like the wind during their entire courtship, if one could call it a courtship.

He didn't know what he was going to do with that crazy little gal. She had certain ideas about how things had been and how they hadn't been—and the funny thing was, she was the mother of his children.

He was going to have to figure this out—fast.

He heard a snuffle from one of the bassinets, a small mewl, and he went to check on Skye. "Hey," he whispered to his daughter, "you want to be picked up?"

The baby let out a tiny noise so he picked her up, nestled her against his chest. And something amazing, something strong, fabulous and true, landed right in his heart, igniting a burning love he'd never experienced before. He held his child, smelled her powdery skin, felt her soft, soft helpless body in his arms, and knew that he'd go to the ends of the earth to be with these children, to protect them, to shelter them, to shield them.

With every last breath in his body.

ASH STARED AT the big sexy cowboy sprawled out on the delicate curved sofa, sound asleep, his boots carefully hanging off Mallory's beloved if old-fashioned furniture. He held Skye against his chest, and the two of them slept peacefully, like two parts of the same body.

Tears jumped into Ash's eyes. Of all the ways she'd imagined Xav interacting with her babies, this wasn't it—and it was better than she could have ever imagined.

She felt her heart spiraling into that same love-struck groove it had always been in where Xav was concerned.

It was the most helpless feeling in the world.

He opened his eyes, smiled at her. "Have a good shower?" he asked softly, so he wouldn't wake the baby.

"I'm a new woman." Ash sat in the chair across from him, the table in between. Mallory had obviously visited with her comfort food, and Xav had partaken. The homey scents of soup and cinnamon drifted to her. "Do you want me to take Skye?"

"She's fine." He stroked his daughter's back. "She's a content little thing once she's picked up and held."

"She's an angel." She looked at her children, all silent for once, a rarity. "I love these babies so much."

"So how'd you end up here?" Xav asked, his gaze piercing as he stared at her. His seen-better-days cowboy hat had slipped forward just a bit as he napped with Skye; he'd probably thought he was lying down for a moment to comfort the baby and didn't think he needed to take it off, then fell asleep. She wanted to remove it for him, smooth the long, dark hair with her fingers.

"Running Bear knew Mallory."

"Of course he did," Xav said. "All these months he kept your location secret from everyone?"

"Grandfather knew I needed to get away. He said I'd be safe here. Mallory's married to a man in law enforcement. He works in another county so I've never met him, but all the local law enforcement and their wives keep a very close eye on Mallory. She's a favorite town daughter." Ash shrugged. "Running Bear said not only would I be safe here, I'd have a mother figure in my life. I said I didn't need one, and he said maybe one day I would."

"So he knew you were pregnant?"

Ash shook her head. "No." She didn't want Xav upset and thinking that the Callahans had been in on a plot to keep him from his children. "Well, no one really ever knows what Running Bear knows. He seems to discern things before anyone else does."

Xav grunted. "I'd like to have known some things about your life, Ashlyn Callahan. About four really small things that should be wearing my last name."

"I don't blame you one bit for feeling that way." Xav was a man of his word, he'd spent several years of his life dedicated to the Callahan cause. "I'm so sorry, Xav. I couldn't tell anyone. And I didn't know I was pregnant with multiples until my ob-gyn here sent me to Houston for a consultation with a doctor who specialized in high-risk pregnancies."

"I would have taken care of you, Ash. Whatever you needed. I wish you'd have let me help you out. I'm sure it was hard to be away from your family while you were pregnant."

It had been. "I was lonely, I'll admit. It was a long time to be confined to a bed. I was often worried about my children." She swallowed. "It was the first time in my life I knew real fear."

"You're a warrior, Ashlyn Callahan. Tough as rocks."

"I know." She smiled a little wistfully. "But even the toughest mother feels a bit helpless when she's not sure if she can bring four babies into the world safely."

"Come sit by Skye. She wants to hold your hand."

She gave the hot cowboy a wry look, knowing very well who wanted to hold her hand. "She's only going to sleep another five minutes. Then she's going to wake up—and so will all of her siblings—and the circus begins again. I suggest you rest up, cowboy. You're going to need your strength."

IF XAV NEEDED STRENGTH, it wasn't for the "baby circus" to which Ash referred. The strength he required was for going slowly, gingerly, trying to fit into her life, instead of trying to make her fit into his desperate wish that she'd marry him.

That conversation hadn't gone off exactly as hoped, with an enthusiastic "Yes, I'll marry you, Xav!"

But he'd been expecting that, and a man who planned well had backup paths to his desired outcome. After the circus—as Ash called it—was completed and the babies were snug in their bassinets and satisfied for the moment, Xav gestured to the babies who lay in the soft glow from the Christmas-tree lights. "I've been thinking, actually the children and I have been thinking. Skye suggests that if her mother is the hunted one, who is destined to bring hellfire and danger to Rancho Diablo and its inhabitants, you're going to need backup. I'm applying for the job. Thorn said he thought it was about time I stepped up, and Briar said a father would make her feel safer than even the Marine Corps at her back. And Valor said it'd be good to turn the responsibility over to me until he's old enough to handle it himself."

Ash stayed far away from him at the other end of the sofa. "You've been conspiring with my children?"

"I've been conspiring with *our* children, yes. And we've come up with quite the remarkable plan. They're very bright, you know."

Ash let out a breath that sounded a bit exasperated. But he thought he was winning her over, because she said, "What is this remarkable plan?"

"You marry me, and we produce a formidable team that faces all challenges together. Including the damnation of being the hunted one." He thought about that for a moment. "I'm still not sure about all the ramifications of that particular designation, but let the record reflect that I face it fearlessly."

"I didn't make the decision to come here lightly. I wouldn't have left Rancho Diablo if I hadn't known that it was best for everyone."

He shrugged. "I didn't make the decision to come here lightly, either. Let's consider you stuck with me."

"That's your marriage proposal?"

"Sure. It'll probably work better with you than the old-fashioned, hearts-and-flowers, on-bended-knee routine."

"Maybe," Ash said, sounding as if she might actually be considering his counterproposal, until the front door crashed open so hard the drapes at the window flew.

"Don't move," Wolf said, "or this time this kid gets it."

He pointed a gun at Skye, and Ash gasped. Wolf's right-hand man, Rhein, slipped in behind his boss, aiming his gun at Ash. "And little mama gets her payback for nearly killing you, Boss."

Xav had never felt so helpless in his life. He'd taken off his holster after entering the house—not wanting to carry when he was around the children. That left him unarmed now, at the worst moment of his life. There was blood in Wolf's eye and he was out for the prize, the biggest Callahan prize of all—the silver-haired only daughter of the Callahan clan—and right then Xav knew that Ash had been right all along.

She was indeed the hunted one.

Chapter Four

"Don't even think about heroics," Wolf said. "Here's where you get lucky. I happen to be in a giving mood tonight. I take my niece, and leave you here alive with these bundles of joy."

Ash looked terrified—and mad—as Rhein held her arms together, quickly binding them with nylon cuffs. Xav feared for her if things got out of control. Ash had a fiery temper and he hoped she didn't unleash it. He started to say, "She's nursing these babies, don't be an idiot, take me instead," then realized he couldn't offer that deal because Wolf didn't know these were Callahan children.

If Wolf knew, he'd be just as likely to kidnap them all.

"You don't want her," Xav said. "Taking her will bring down Callahan wrath on you."

"I know what I'm doing. Thanks, though, for the generous advice." Wolf jerked his head at Rhein to depart with Ash. She kicked Rhein in the shin, and he slapped her. Xav grit his teeth, reminding himself that the patient man left himself the most options.

"If you call the law, we'll kill her," Wolf said, waving his gun for emphasis.

"You'd kill your own niece," Xav stated, his voice deadly quiet. Wolf had a hair-trigger temper as the door hanging by a hinge illustrated. He'd been spoiling for revenge for months.

"I probably will anyway, but that's not your concern." He glanced at the babies in the bassinets, sleeping soundly for the moment, thankfully. "Let me tell you how this is going to go down. This isn't about you, it doesn't concern you. If you come after us, we'll shoot her on the spot. But if you give us an hour's head start, she'll live. Best deal I'll offer you. Don't make me have to shoot you, too," Wolf said. "I'm kind of in a killing mood, to be honest. In case you don't know, my dear angelic niece nearly killed me. She and I have things to talk about, but that's none of your business." He stared Xav down. "You get me?"

"I do. One hour head start, no more."

"That's all I need for the party I'm planning." Wolf followed Rhein to his black truck.

Mallory peeked around the corner. "What is going on?"

"Just an unforeseen event that requires a bit of attention. Can you move the babies to the back of the house, quickly?"

Mallory grabbed up a baby, then another, and scrambled down the hall. Xav didn't move, but watched Ash put up a helluva fight as Rhein and Wolf tried to get her into the truck. Mallory had the other two babies moved while Ash struggled, and Xav got his gun from the holster he'd laid on the sofa, unlocked it and checked the magazine.

"Do you want me to call the sheriff?" Mallory whispered from the kitchen.

"In a minute you're going to hear two shots. After the second shot, you can call the sheriff."

"Okay."

He heard the kitchen door close and trained his eyes on Ash. Rhein and Wolf had finally managed to wrangle her into the truck, and were driving away when suddenly she fell out of the vehicle and started to run toward the woods across the street. The truck stopped and Wolf and Rhein ran after her, and from the front door, Xav fired once, twice.

He smiled.

Ash whirled to stare at him from two hundred yards away. Her hands were still bound. She bent down to stare at her uncle and gave Rhein a cursory glance. Stomping toward the house, she met him on the porch, her eyes blazing.

"You killed him!"

Xav shrugged. "He said he was in a killing mood. I decided to take care of his mood."

"Running Bear said no one was to harm his son!"

He stared at the silver-haired spitfire he adored from her small feet to her big, wide navy eyes—Callahan eyes. "Your grandfather said none of you Callahans were to harm him. Mc, I'm not a Callahan. I'm a Phillips. And as your uncle so clearly pointed out, his problem had nothing to do with me." He tugged Ash to him, removing his knife from his boot to cut her free. "Now, the mother of my children has everything to do with me. There was no way on this planet I was going to let him drag off my babies' mother."

Ash slowly nodded and drew a shaky breath. "Thank you."

He enveloped her in his arms. "I take it you're not going to fire me, Callahan?"

She sniffled against his chest, and he realized his

nerves-of-steel lady was shaken, frightened. He decided it was best not to injure her pride by commenting on her tears. Stroking her back, he let her know she was safe.

"Where are the babies?" she asked, her voice slightly unsteady.

"Safe in the nice warm kitchen with Mallory. She's called the sheriff. You should go take a bath, try to relax." He ran a hand down her long blond ponytail.

She drew in a hiccup breath. "I think I'll go call Running Bear."

"Even better idea." The chief would calm Ash down, relieve her anxiety. She disappeared, and as the sun began setting in the sky, sending the gray of winter into the living room, Xav glanced at the empty bassinets and thought how lucky it was that he'd found Ash when he had. Things could have turned out so differently if Wolf had gotten here before he did.

But knowing the chief the way he did, the timing was probably no accident at all.

"THERE'RE NO BODIES anywhere out there," Sheriff Lopez said thirty minutes later. He and his deputies had scoured the fields and woods across the way, returning to the house to make their report. "Are you sure you hit them? Because we find no evidence of blood or any type of struggle."

Ash and Xav shared a startled glance. "I know they were dead," Ash told the sheriff. "I'm sure Rhein was. And Wolf didn't look very lively."

They stood inside at the fireplace, warming themselves as the sheriff wrote up their statements. She'd offered him some hot cocoa, which he'd accepted gratefully. The weather outdoors was a bone-chilling fifteen degrees, and the sheriff and his men had been searching for Wolf and Rhein with no luck. Now it was dark—solidly black outside the big window. The Christmas-tree lights twinkled with soft color, but Ash didn't feel any sense of holiday peace.

Not now.

"I shot both of them." Xav leaned against the mantel, stared down at the fire. "I didn't aim to merely wound. I saw them hit the ground."

"Well, it's a mystery," Sheriff Lopez said, his tone cheerful for a man who'd been out hunting for dead thugs. "You should get some sleep, Ash. I'm sure those four angels of yours keep you quite busy."

He tipped his hat to her, thanked her for the cocoa, told her to say goodbye to Mallory for him and slipped out the front door. She turned to Xav who studied her with his dark, intense gaze.

"That's odd. Don't you think? There's no way the bodies weren't out there," Ash said.

"I know. I don't understand it."

She wanted to walk into Xav's arms and stay there forever. She couldn't. He'd killed two men because of her. She *had* brought darkness and devastation to him, just as Running Bear's warning had foretold. "You'd never killed anyone before, had you?" she asked, destroyed by the knowledge he'd crossed a place in his soul he could never return from because of her.

"That's not something I'm going to discuss."

"You shouldn't bear that because of me, because of my family."

"I don't bear anything, Ash. Two armed men entered your home with full intent to kidnap you. Perhaps they would have returned for the children." He shrugged.

"If there was a burden for me to bear, it would have been calling your brothers and telling them I'd let Wolf kidnap you. He clearly intended to harm you. I feel no burden at all. Besides which, your brothers don't even know that you've had children. If they knew that you'd just been attacked, this place would be swarming with Callahans rushing to protect their sister. No, I feel no burden at all, just a sense of peace."

"I don't feel peace." She glanced toward the window, at the darkness shrouding the house. "I feel unsettled. It didn't take the sheriff but maybe thirty minutes to get here. What happened to the bodies?"

"I don't know." He pulled her into his arms and she went willingly. "But they were dead, Ash. They're not ever coming back to hurt you or the children."

"I know." Goose pimples ran over her arms just the same, and a dizzying sense of worry swept her.

"I thought some potato soup and hot apple cider might be the thing to settle everyone's nerves," Mallory said, poking her head into the room. "Oh, the sheriff's gone. Let me bring you two something to eat."

"Thank you," Ash said, glad for the interruption even if she didn't feel like eating. Anything to feel like life was normal, and not a horrible nightmare from which she couldn't wake.

"I would swear I've seen Mallory somewhere before," Xav said, staring after the older woman. "I have the strangest feeling I know her."

"You're from Texas. Were you ever in Wild?"

"No. Kendall, Gage, Shaman and I have been through lots of the state with Gil Phillips, Inc., but somehow we never made it to Wild."

"Maybe she reminds you of someone you met." Ash

left his arms and went to the tray to pour a cup of cider for him and one for her. "She's been very good to me. Motherly, in a way."

"I'm glad." He sat across from her, took the mug she handed him. "What did Running Bear say when you called him?"

"That things happen the way they are meant to. That I should take care of the babies now."

"He wants you to return to Rancho Diablo?"

"We didn't discuss it. But I know it's time." Ash wanted her brothers to meet their new nieces and nephews; she wanted to hug Fiona and Burke. She'd been so homesick, though she wouldn't say that out loud. "I'd like to be home for Christmas."

"Consider my truck your sleigh, then," Xav said, and Ash nodded, glad that her children's father could be with them.

But she had a niggling feeling she'd brought darkness to Xav's soul.

MALLORY CAME OUT to say goodbye, and help them put the babies in the SUV the sheriff had lent Ash and Xav to get home with their babies.

"I'll miss them," Mallory said.

"Come with us," Ash said. "I could certainly use the help." She would miss Mallory, too, and terribly so. The two of them had grown close during the months they'd spent together.

"I would love to come with you," Mallory said, "but I'm better staying here. Feel free to return whenever you want to. Holidays, weekends, weekdays, whenever."

Ash smiled and hugged Mallory. "I'll remember that."

"Keep up the fight," Mallory whispered against her ear. "The fight is all that matters. And remember that so often what we think we see hides what we really should be seeing."

Ash hesitated. "The fight?"

Mallory pulled away and thrust a bag into Ash's hands. "These are snacks for the road. You'll find just about everything one needs for good nutrition between here and Rancho Diablo without having to stop for fast food." She smiled at Xav. "Thank you for keeping an eye on Ashlyn. She's very special to me."

"You won't be worried to stay here by yourself?" Xav asked Mallory. Ash watched his gaze sweep the property before he shook Mallory's hand.

"No. I'm not afraid. All is well with me here. Drive safely. Let me know when you arrive."

They got in the truck, waved goodbye. "I don't know what I'll do without her," Ash said.

"I know. She treats you like a long-lost daughter." Xav started the truck and drove off. They waved to Mallory as she stood on the porch, watching them go.

"She said something about keeping up the fight," Ash said. The rest of Mallory's words echoed in her head, but she didn't repeat them. "She'll be safe, won't she?"

"Sure. The sheriff will keep a tight eye on her."

"I don't understand where the bodies went. It worries me." Mallory's life had been uncomplicated before the Callahans had arrived.

"She'll call if she needs help. She has my cell number."

Ash looked at Xav, grateful for his calm strength. "Thanks."

"No problem." He glanced at her. "Are you all right?"

"Yes. Just a little worried about Mallory."

"She knew what she was getting into when Running Bear asked her if you could stay there, babe."

"I wish she'd come with us."

He put his hand over hers, lightly squeezing her fingers. "We'll bring the babies back to see her soon."

She looked at him. "Thank you for understanding. And for being here."

It felt strange to be in a car with Xav, with their four children, considering the many years she'd spent chasing after him. "You know, in all the years I've know you, you never asked me out."

A smile creased his nicely shaped lips, lips that Ash had loved kissing, wanted to kiss now. "You're right. I didn't."

"Why not?" For so long she'd despaired of ever "catching" Xav. "It always felt like you were avoiding me."

"I was." He laughed at her gasp. "I could see no good reason to allow my employer's wild little sister to seduce me. And it was clear that was what was on your mind."

"I don't know that you put up *that* much of a fight."

He laughed. "I liked letting you catch me, I'm not going to lie."

She arched a brow. "I don't believe for a moment that you were afraid of my brothers."

"Not afraid. Wary. Then again, I was faced with one tiny, loud, adorable lady who had a penchant for lovemaking while I was on duty. What's a guy to do?"

Ash looked out the window. "Exactly what you did."

"That's right. And now I plan to marry you, make an honest woman of you. I'm not sure that's entirely possible, but we'll give it our best shot."

"I never agreed to that."

"You will," he said cheerfully, "or no more love-making for you."

She turned to him. "That's your best bargaining chip?"

"It was good enough to get you into the canyons, beautiful, it'll be good enough to get you to say 'I do.'"

"We'll see," Ash said.

"Yes, we will," Xav said, and kissed her hand like an old-fashioned prince in her personal fairy tale.

But he wasn't. He'd shot her uncle and his thug, and they'd disappeared. He'd done that for her, and nothing was right about the price he'd had to pay for her.

She needed to talk to Running Bear in the worst way. Only he would understand that she couldn't bring evil to her own family, and certainly not to the man she loved.

Chapter Five

Xav and Ash spent the night in the first town they hit in New Mexico, but staying in a hotel with four babies proved to be an experience Xav didn't want to repeat. The entire time they were there Xav had the eerie feeling they were being watched, and he had no good way to protect his family.

Glad as he was to finally arrive at Rancho Diablo, he was somewhat apprehensive about facing the Callahans. According to Ash, she hadn't told them about the fact that she was pregnant when she'd left Rancho Diablo, nor that she'd had four children—and they didn't know he'd killed Wolf. The conversation was destined to be Callahan crazy. Xav took a deep breath and looked around, trying to decide if he felt as if he was at home, or in the enemy camp.

He'd know soon enough.

The stunning Tudor-style house with the seven chimneys had always seemed like something out of a legendary tale, a backdrop to the immense beauty of New Mexico. As comfortable as his own compound at Hell's Colony was—where the Callahan cousins currently resided with their many children for safekeeping, and several of the Chacon Callahan wives and children, too—his statuesque mansion always struck Xav as nothing short of an architectural ode to freedom and spirit. Now Sloan, Falcon, Tighe, Tighe's twin, Dante, Jace and Galen Chacon Callahan eyed him as Sloan handed him a whiskey in the beautiful upstairs library where the family meetings were always held—his first time to be included.

He almost thought the gesture felt a little ominous, but since he'd texted the brothers to say he was coming home with their sister and would like to request a meeting, maybe they were giving him a courtesy by inviting him into the vaunted private area.

The Callahan brothers took seats on the fine dark leather sofas and looked at him expectantly.

"So, you called this meeting," Galen said. "We were a little surprised you returned. Hell, we were surprised that you left. Didn't know you'd left to find our sister until Fiona finally told us."

"I did give notice of my departure," Xav reminded the brothers.

"Yes," Tighe said, "but you didn't say you were going to find Ash. We figured you were going to visit your family."

"Or take a well-deserved vacation." Jace grinned. "Actually, we figured you were going off for a major bender. Or had found a new lady you—"

"No," Xav said, interrupting to head off that train of thought. Crap, why would they imagine he was looking at anyone besides their sister? He hadn't since the moment he first saw her. If he counted the years he'd been in love with Ash and waited to have her, he'd certainly put in enough time to grow a beard to his boots.

"I did not go off on a bender or with a woman. I went to bring Ash home, as Fiona asked."

There was general nodding from the brothers. Fiona's wish was typically her command, and when she gave one everyone jumped. Xav swallowed the whiskey, realizing the atmosphere was tense. Perhaps best to change the subject. "Maybe you've heard through the grapevine that I shot Wolf. And Rhein."

Falcon nodded. "We did hear about that from Ash."

The room was very still; no one moved. Xav swallowed uncomfortably. He didn't know if they'd thank him or tell him he'd crossed some huge Callahan boundary. "I know the rule that governs you where Wolf was concerned, but I had no choice. They were kidnapping Ash." His blood still boiled at the memory.

The Callahans wore grave expressions, displeased by the threat to their beloved sister. He heard a few muttered curse words, some dire venting of temper soaked up by whiskey sipping.

"The problem is, they disappeared," Xav said. "Wolf and Rhein were dead, as far as I could tell. But when the sheriff went to find them, he said he couldn't locate the bodies."

"It doesn't make sense," Dante said. "It worries me."

"You got off clean shots?" Galen asked.

"They were taking Ash," Xav said, his jaw tensing. "I wasn't going to let that happen. The shots were clean."

"Ash says they definitely looked dead." Tighe shrugged. "Ash would know."

He'd aimed to kill. "They were as dead as I could make them," Xav said flatly. "Unless they're immortal."

"Then you did your job well," Jace said. "For that we thank you."

"Do we?" Sloan asked. "Besides the fact that he didn't let our sister get kidnapped—which I have no doubt would have ended very badly for all—we were told by Grandfather not to kill his son."

"Xav's only a Callahan in spirit," Falcon said. "Whatever Running Bear is worried about should not apply to Xav."

"Okay," Galen said, "so why have you returned?"

The question surprised Xav. "Why wouldn't Ash want to return to Rancho Diablo? It's the Christmas season. She's been gone almost a year."

"Yes," Galen said, "but it's still not safe here."

"Tell your sister that," Xav said. "I went to go get her, true, but she wanted to come home after Wolf—" He stopped, not really sure how to proceed. "Why did Ash tell you she wanted to come home?"

"She said you found her, asked her to marry you," Sloan said. "She says she doesn't want to marry you."

They looked quite defensive of their sister, and not impressed with his offer of marriage. If he hadn't expected some blowback, he might have wilted a bit in the face of this lack of enthusiasm for his marriage suit.

But one expected tricky curves in the road from the Callahans. They were totally unpredictable—and proud of it.

"Look, your sister's in a difficult spot right now."

"But you do want to marry her?" Falcon asked.

"Of course I do!" Xav glared at the men who would be his brothers-in-law. "Didn't you want to marry the mother of your offspring?"

They all looked at him curiously.

"Offspring?" Dante asked. "Has something sprung?"

"What is an offspring, anyway?" Tighe asked his twin. "Offspring. That word makes no sense. It has nothing to do with babies, or children, or anything else." He looked at Xav. "Ash has no offspring, if you clumsily mean children."

Xav blinked at his employers. "Ash drew a four of a kind when you fellows weren't looking."

"Four of a kind?" Jace looked perplexed. "Ash doesn't play poker. She can play a mean hand of old maid, but she prefers chess as a rule."

Xav wondered if they were deliberately being obtuse, joshing him about his new dad status. The Callahans were known to be tricksters, and nobody loved playing a practical joke more than they did.

He realized with some approbation that as Ash had been driving the truck when they'd finally made it back to Rancho Diablo, she'd dropped him off out in front of the house, saying that Fiona was waiting for her in the kitchen. Fiona could help her with the babies and Ash asked Xav to go find her brothers to let them know she was home. Her brothers would likely be scattered around the ranch, and texts would need to be sent, she'd said. Besides, she wanted to walk in the back door where the scent of Fiona's baking would be in the kitchen, one of her fondest memories.

Xav had agreed, and gone to start locating Callahans, a job anyone knew could be like herding cats. "Didn't you talk to Ash?"

"She sent a group text, said you were calling a meeting, which we already knew from your text." Galen shrugged. "We figured something had to be up. Right now, we just want to see her. Where the hell is she?"

That little minx. She'd told him to hunt up her brothers, then pulled a disappearing act. She'd sent him on a fool's errand to give her time to sneak in the house. She had no intention of being the one to tell her brothers she had four babies. She was going to let him be the bearer of shocking news—and put one over on her brothers. Xav frowned. "The race for that ranch land across the canyons was called off, wasn't it? Didn't you buy all that land?" he asked Galen.

"Loco Diablo?" Galen nodded. "I bought it, and then I parceled it out to my siblings, including Ash. She doesn't know yet because she's been gone. Nobody gets their share until they have a family, according to Fiona's dictates, so Ash's is still being held in trust until she marries. Why do you ask? Thinking of proposing properly?"

"I have proposed properly! About a hundred times!" What was wrong with these thickheaded Callahans? Didn't they understand that he was crazy about their sister? "She won't marry me. We have four children together, but your sister has a thousand reasons, most of them superstitious mumbo jumbo, in my opinion, to avoid giving my children my name!"

They stared at him blankly.

"Babies?" Dante said. "You said a four of a kind. You didn't say Ash had babies. Is that what you're trying to say in a rather ham-handed fashion?"

"Ash and I are the parents of four beautiful babies," Xav said, slowly, enunciating, so they could understand that this was a moment for celebration and not for being thick as milk shakes.

"Four?" Jace guffawed. He clapped Xav on the back. "Nice try. Our sister doesn't have four children. That would make her the outright winner of Loco Diablo.

It would mean our tiny little sister, who couldn't be tamed if someone spent years trying, is a mother. The whole thing is so impossible that if it were true, we'd basically have to give her Loco Diablo as an homage to her accomplishment. Four children! Ha-ha-ha," Jace said, obviously very amused and well pleased with his jibe at Xav.

The brothers chuckled, eyed Xav with patient, laughing eyes. As if he was simple as a stone.

Galen shook his head. "Where would Ash get four children? And is that why you asked about Loco Diablo? You hoping for a cut, slick?"

He was so close to punching his employers in their Callahan noses.

"While we appreciate you taking care of our sister and doing the deed on Uncle Wolf, we don't give out land," Falcon said. "It's not ours to give. It's really our Callahan cousins, as is this house, because they'd get a vote in anything that happens here. We consider ourselves merely warriors."

"In fact," Tighe said, "if Uncle Wolf is really dead, our cousins can come home. And we can move on!"

They all stared at each other, realization sinking in.

"My God, we're free," Sloan said.

"Free," Dante repeated. "Thanks to you, Xav."

"Is anyone listening?" Xav demanded. "I'm in love with your sister, and I want to marry her, and we have four children, and no, I don't want your stupid land, but I could use some backup here! Little sister isn't gonna be exactly easy to drag to the altar, and I assume you'd like her married now that she's a mother!"

"Whoa," Sloan said. "Easy, brother."

"Chill," Falcon said. "Let your spirit be calm."

"Deep breaths," Tighe said. "Breathe from the air which blesses us."

"Think of yourself as spirit, untroubled, free," Dante said, his voice hypnotic.

"Have some more whiskey," Jace said, topping off his crystal tumbler.

"Meditate," Galen said. "Meditation is the key to a peaceful soul."

Xav sank back into the leather. "You're all certifiable. Nutty as fruitcakes."

Ash walked into the library, and her brothers stared at the huge stroller she rolled in front of her. "Thank heaven for the secret elevator," she announced. "I can't run up and down the stairs all day with four babies."

The brothers rushed to stare down into the stroller and hug their sister. She was surrounded by big, musclebound Callahans, and Xav could barely see her platinum hair through the meatheaded scrum engulfing her.

"Holy crap," Sloan said. "There's four babies in here!"

"Two boys, two girls," Falcon said. "That's not a four of a kind, it's two pair. Still pretty good. Competitive, even."

"Where'd you get four babies, Ash?" Jace asked. "Are we babysitting?"

"They're mine, doofuses," Ash told her brothers fondly. "What do you think?"

They looked her up and down, glanced at Xav who grinned proudly. "What did I tell you?" Xav asked.

"You didn't tell us this," Dante said, and Xav shook his head. Dante looked at his sister. "Ash, what the hell? These can't be your babies!"

His twin agreed. "If these babies were yours, you would have notified us at once that we were uncles. You're pulling our legs."

"And they don't look like you," Sloan said. "They're beautiful."

Ash popped Sloan on the arm. "Pick up a baby and quit being a weenie. All of you. Babies, meet your uncles. You'll meet lightbulbs brighter than them in your lifetimes, but they're more softhearted than softheaded."

Galen gingerly picked up Skye. "Ash, what the hell?" he asked, dumbfounded. "When did this happen?"

"It happened over a period of about eight months," Ash said, watching with pride as her knuckleheaded brothers began jostling with each other to see who could grab a baby and who would get left out.

Xav watched the clown act and decided he could use one last small topper on his whiskey. "This is some homecoming," he told Ash. "Did you realize your brothers are uniformly dysfunctional?"

She laughed. "We're all dysfunctional. You know that by now."

"Yeah, but I thought there'd be, you know, cigars. High fives. Huzzahs." He thought Ash was the most beautiful woman he'd ever seen in his life, and he couldn't believe this wonderful woman had borne his children. "They can't get it through their leather-tough scalps that I want to marry you. Like, today."

"Marriage!" the Callahans said, and Xav found himself the target of six pairs of navy-blue eyes.

"You want to marry him, Ash?" Sloan asked. "Because if you don't, we'll run him off for you."

"Even if he did take out our worst enemy, we won't let him hang around," Falcon said, "if you don't want him."

"Don't feed him," Dante said. "That's the key. If you don't feed him, he'll move on."

"Or expire," Tighe said.

Xav's lips folded as he listened to the nonsense spouting from the Callahans. "Of course Ash is going to marry me. I just need your permission to formally ask her for her hand in marriage."

"Well, now," Galen said, his chest puffing a bit, "we'll have to have a family meeting to talk it over."

"This *is* a family meeting," Xav pointed out.

"No," Jace said, "you're here, dude. And you're not family. Yet."

"You guys are being mean to the father of my children," Ash said, laughing. "Xav, they're just teasing you."

Xav looked at the Callahans warily. "Teasing?"

The brothers burst out laughing. "Yeah, we're teasing you," Dante said. "We're not saying Ash will marry you or anything, so don't get excited. We were going to make you repeat your proposal about a hundred times, and then tell you we'd arranged a marriage for Ash. We wanted to see that famous cool of yours melt like a snowman in Fiona's oven."

He hadn't been cool since he'd found out he was a dad. The Callahans laughed like hyenas at their practical joke, came over and pounded him on the back. Xav thought he was going to cough up a lung.

"Dude, if you're going to be part of the family, you're going to have to get with the program," Tighe said.

"Yeah, we stay loose around here," Sloan said.

"Oh, good grief," Ash said, "you're only loose in your brains. Someone give him his cigar, his new dad shirt and his Callahan badge of honor."

Xav felt better now that he realized he'd been part of some colossal ribbing. Jace dragged out a bottle of fine whiskey, handed it to Xav with great fanfare.

"Congratulations," Galen said. "You win the prize."

"See what four of a kind gets you?" Falcon said.

"It's two pair, nothing to get excited about," Tighe said, staring down at baby Thorn in his arms. "These babies look like their mother, thank God."

They grinned as a pack. Xav glanced at Ash. "Now that I've survived the Callahan gauntlet, I want to hear yes out of you," he said to Ash. "'Yes, Xav, you studly fellow' would work for me."

Ash snorted and sat on a sofa, watched her brothers handling her babies, cooing to them and making puppet faces with wide mouths and pop eyes. Xav thought they looked ridiculous but totally happy. Fiona came in silently, snapping photos like mad before anyone realized the family meeting had been breached by the intrepid aunt.

"We have a lot to discuss," Ash said. "Planning a wedding's going to have to wait. First on the agenda is finding out what happened to Wolf."

"How can we find that out?" Xav asked. "No stall tactics, please. Callahans, will you please tell your sister that the children you're holding deserve a father? My last name? This is a very serious matter."

Galen raised his head. "Something wrong with Chacon Callahan for a last name?"

"Yes, there is, damn it," Xav said. "It's not my name, and I'm the father."

"He does have a point," Sloan said. "You have to give him credit for making an important point."

"We give him credit," Jace said, "but not our sister."

Xav sighed. "I feel like I'm talking to Jell-O that keeps sliding around."

Falcon shook his head. "Exaggeration and hyperbole is no way to make your case."

"True," Tighe said. "You're going to have to do better than that."

"Why should we let you marry our sister?" Sloan asked.

"Wait a darn minute," Ash said. "While I appreciate you doing the courteous thing by asking my brothers for my hand, you're going about this all wrong," she told Xav. "They'll put you through the wringer before they ever say yes. Don't go down a hard path, for your own sanity." She glared at her six brothers. "Besides which, I make my own decisions on whom I'm going to marry, thank you all very little for overdoing the brother act."

"It was fun," Dante said. "Kind of wish you wouldn't make us quit."

"Not fun for me," Xav said. "I've been through a lot to catch this woman."

"*You've* been through a lot? Try carrying quadruplets and then birthing them and nursing them," Ash said.

"Look, I just want to marry you," Xav said. "No matter what quest I have to go on, you're going to be my wife. We're going to be a family, you, me, Thorn, Skye, Briar and Valor."

"Man," Jace said, looking at his sister, "you probably better let him off the hook. I remember the feeling, and it sucks when you can't get the girl."

"Really stinks," Galen said, "but we did say you'd be the worst one to tie down, Ash. It's coming true."

"I'm not trying to be difficult," Ash said. "I'm trying to tell you that I can't get married. I'm the hunted one."

They stared at their sister, and Xav watched their faces practically droop with astonished concern.

"No, you're not, Ash," Galen said, his tone big-brother comforting. "You're not the one who brings the curse."

"No," Sloan said, "it's…" His gaze flew wildly around the room. "Well, obviously it's Dante because he's crazy as a bedbug, anyway."

"Probably it's Tighe," Dante said. "My twin put the bad word on all of us. Remember? He spoke into the wind that he hoped we'd all go hard into the marriage chase, and we did. It was hard as hell on every last one of us."

"Not in front of the aunt, please," Galen said. "Fiona, tell Ash she's not the hunted one."

Fiona wandered out the door. "I'll bring chocolate chip cookies up," she called over her shoulder.

Ash's brothers stared at her silently. Xav reached over and took her hand. "Babe, it's going to be all right. I've got your back on this hunted thing."

"You can't fight things you don't understand."

"No, but I did shoot your uncle, and I'm living large on those laurels for now," Xav said cheerfully. "Now, where's my dad badge you said you had for me?"

Chapter Six

"That was mean," Ash said, after Xav left with the children to visit Fiona and Burke and put the babies to bed. She'd said she was going to do it, but Xav wanted to find out where Fiona thought would be best for them all to sleep, wheeling the enormous stroller/pram out of the library. The stroller was a Callahan hand-me-down, and she loved it already. Burke had invented it by combining two double-strollers, so that all babies had plenty of room to nest in blankets or ride when they were a bit older. There were usually scads of Callahan babies around Rancho Diablo, so the stroller was almost never out of service. But transporting babies was the least of her worries at the moment. "You guys can't pick on Xav like that."

"Are you going to marry him?" Jace asked. "Because if you are, you might want to tell him so he can quit holding his breath. He seems a bit gaunt around the eyes, like a dog with a juicy bone just out of reach."

"Agreed," Sloan said. "Did we have it that bad?"

"Nah," Falcon said. "We were all in control of our emotions where our women were concerned."

Ash waited for a big, windy guffaw from her brothers at the exaggerated bragging, but when none came, she realized they really believed they'd been in control of the women in their lives. And their destinies. "Whatever. But you can't just gang up on Xav."

"So you are going to marry him," Tighe said. "You sound like you're in love."

"I do love him, and no, I'm not going to marry him. Have you been listening? He shot Wolf because of me. Nothing good can come of this." She shook her head. "If we were all being honest, we would tell Xav right now that witness protection is the place for him."

They stared at her in silence, then looked down. Up at the ceiling. At the cookies Fiona had quietly brought in before departing without saying a word. They looked anywhere but at her.

Chickens.

"She's right," Galen said, sounding defeated. "Xav's going to have to go into hiding, and witness protection might even be advisable."

"I don't want to tell him," Dante finally said. "He's going to punch the bearer of that bad news. Hard."

They considered their dilemma. Ash could feel her heart get heavier by the moment. How was it possible that the man she loved with all her soul needed to be in hiding? She had chased Xav endlessly for years, her spirit following his, knowing that he was the only man she could ever feel so strongly about.

Yet to protect her, he'd done what none of them would do. And would pay a terrible price.

"He won't go," Jace said. "I don't care what we say to him, Xav isn't going into witness protection."

"He knows our story," Dante said. "He knows we were raised without our parents in the tribe. That our cousins were mostly raised without theirs. He knows what it cost our family. He came here willingly because of that cost, because he wanted to help. I agree with Jace. Xav won't go anywhere."

Ash shook her head, not wanting to hear the words, and yet her heart leaped just the same. She didn't want to lose him. She didn't want her children growing up without their father. She thought about her babies' sweet faces and their tiny little bodies. When they lay against her, she could feel their heartbeats, and fierce love swept her. She'd do anything to protect her children, keep them safe.

No doubt her parents had felt that very same emotion about her and her brothers. Hot determination poured through her, making her strong.

"You could go with him," Galen said, his voice quiet.

No one said a word. They got up, went to face the windows that overlooked the ranch now wrapped in darkness, frost on the windowpanes, the smell of cocoa drifting up from downstairs. They stood close to their sister, shielding her, and she felt their support of whatever decision she had to make.

Suddenly the sound of pounding hooves rose on the air, a distant, rhythmic music they'd heard many times.

"The Diablos," Galen murmured. "They've returned."

Legend had it that the spirit horses were a mystical portent of things to come. Wolf had wanted the Diablos, the very spirit of their home. He'd even trapped them at one point, determined to steal the very heart of the Callahan wealth. The cartel that hired Wolf wanted the Callahan parents, Jeremiah and Molly, dead, and the Chacon Callahan parents, Carlos and Julia, dead, as well. Wolf had sold his brothers Carlos and Jeremiah out to the cartel, determined to have their land, the fabled silver treasure, and the Diablos. Running Bear despaired of his son Wolf but was proud of his sons Carlos and Jeremiah, proud that they'd understood the heritage of the land and fought the good fight. What affected Rancho Diablo also affected the homespun, tight-knit town of Diablo, and Jeremiah and Carlos had long ago made the decision that they couldn't allow the cartel and Wolf to destroy the town and its people, as well. Livelihoods would have been ruined, families moved away, and the community fabric would have been ripped apart. Here would lie a barren wasteland if not for the sacrifices their parents had made.

Now Ash had decisions to make. Just because Wolf was gone didn't mean Rancho Diablo was safe.

A chill touched her skin as she saw the future laid out before her, hanging in the distance like a mirage, bleak and bare, the echo of the pounding hooves reminding her that the war had not been won.

Yet.

"THE THING IS, ASH," Xav said, staring down at his tiny bundles of joy as they slept peacefully in their bassinettes. They had all been placed in the bunkhouse at the end of Rancho Diablo, nearest the canyons. "The thing is, I was a reluctant suitor. I freely admit that."

Ash smiled at Thorn, adjusting his diaper. The baby slept on, wiped out because of the crying jag he'd just experienced. Thorn seemed prone to those, but Xav didn't mind the late-afternoon crying spells; it was proof to him that the underdeveloped lungs his son had been born with were a thing of the past.

"Ash," Xav said, "I'm not a reluctant suitor anymore."

She looked at him, and he thought he'd never seen eyes with such depth that could knock him to his knees. "It's enough to know you care, Xav."

Care? He loved this sexily stubborn woman. "Yeah, well, it's time we get married. These children need to be christened. A house needs to be bought. Schools need to be chosen. We'll of course need to visit colleges and military schools as soon as possible so the kids can get an idea of their future."

Ash shook her head. "We have different plans to make."

That sounded better—at least his little darling was in a planning mood, and indicated that she intended to include him. "Go for it. I'm listening."

"You need to go away, Xav," she said softly, and his heart turned over, fell to the ground, flailed like a dying thing.

"Go away?"

"I'm afraid so."

He saw tears glimmer in her eyes, and realized she was dead serious. "I'm not going anywhere, babe. Those are my children, and you're my…my dream come true. That may sound kind of sappy but sappy's good sometimes."

"You're going to have to go into hiding."

She didn't sound sappy at all, she sounded very direct, clearheaded and matter-of-fact. "I don't think so. I'm not a hiding kind of guy. I'm an up-front-and-personal kind of guy. Where you go, I go."

"Then maybe that's the answer," Ash said, her voice very, very quiet. "Maybe we go away. All of us."

He sat next to her. "What's going on? Do your brothers want you to run me out of town on a rail?"

"Something's going to have to happen."

"This is going to happen," he said, and kissed her, taking his sweet time about it, the memories of their lovemaking crashing down on him. This was where he belonged, with her, and nothing was ever going to separate them. Nothing.

Her lips pressed against his, kissing him passionately and his heart sang with joy, with a realization that all the months apart had done nothing to change the way they were together. "If you're trying to seduce me into something, it's probably working," Xav said, "unless you're trying to seduce me into agreeing to leave you, and then that's not going to happen. Fair warning."

She sat on his lap facing him, her legs behind his back. He thought he might explode from the desire screaming through him.

"What's going on, little lady? You're going dangerous places."

Ash looked in his eyes. "I'm going in your bed right now. We'll talk later about what you don't want to talk about."

"Oh, no, you don't. Not that it doesn't kill me to say that." He kissed her again. "You think lovemaking is the way to my heart after nine long months, and it is. So the answer's no, beautiful." He put her off his lap, and his body—and wiser parts of him—complained vigorously.

She got right back in his lap, and he didn't have the strength to remove her again. There was only so much a man could stand when a woman had seduction on her mind, and he was a very weak man when it came to Ashlyn Callahan.

She darn well knew it.

"Xav, I'm not going to beg."

"No, probably I'll be doing the begging, and I really have no problem doing it, either." He sighed, kissed her, thought about his options, realized his little lady was trying to sidetrack him from some serious decisions. "Ash, I'm not going to leave you, the babies or Rancho Diablo."

"Okay."

He raised his brows. "Just like that."

"Yes. Now let's get in bed."

"While you sound very much more like the hot lady that liked to make love to me when we were dating—"

She leaned back to look at him. "Dating? We didn't date. I chased you and you ran like a little girl."

He laughed. "Not a little girl, surely."

"A scared rabbit."

"I wasn't afraid of making love to you, gorgeous."

"Really? I spent at least four years sure that that was exactly what you were afraid of. Every time I caught you, you ran a little farther away again."

He nibbled on her shoulder. "Made it all that much better for you when you caught me, though, didn't it?"

"Not necessarily."

A baby squeaked in its bassinet and they both looked over at Briar. "I think you're bothering our children, my love," Xav said.

She took off her blouse, and his heart practically stopped beating. "Holy Christmas. Dressed for the holidays, babe?" He stared at the red lacy bra barely covering her nipples.

"You could say that. And there's matching panties, if you can remember your way."

He was having trouble breathing. "Ash, I really think we need to talk this out. You haven't been yourself since I

told you that it was me who shot your uncle at Rancho—"
His words stopped and his breath choked off as she got
out of his lap and dropped her short black leather skirt
to the floor. She hadn't been exaggerating—a red lace
valentine stared at him, and she turned slowly, letting
him see that her fanny cheeks were bare, beautiful, and
sweetly divided by a sexy red lace thong.

Okay, so there was going to be no more talking tonight.

He snatched Ash up, cradled her in his arms.

"Change your mind?" she asked, her voice oh-too-
innocent.

"Strangely enough, I have."

He sank into bed with his prize, made short work of
the hot lingerie, felt his whole body sigh with the relief of having her back in his arms again. "God, this is
good," he said with a bone-deep sigh, inhaling her per-
fume and the scent of her skin. "I missed the hell out
of you. This is better than good."

"We haven't done anything yet," she said, her voice
teasing.

She thought she was so smart, thought she had his
number.

She did.

And he was crazy about her.

"Did you tell him?" Dante asked Ash the next day as
she walked into the kitchen to grab two mugs of coffee.

It was two weeks until Christmas. All she wanted
was the joy of being home with her family, to celebrate
the holidays the way only a family could—together.
They'd worked so hard for this for so long. And she had
these beautiful babies to be thankful for, a miracle that

she could never have envisioned. The babies had been bathed, fed and dressed in darling soft, warm, matching pajamas. They'd looked like tiny candy canes in their bassinets when she'd left them, slumbering with their big, handsome father. "No. I didn't tell him. I tried to tell Xav he had to go, but the discussion got waylaid." Ash smiled to herself, remembering how Xav had loved her—and then loved her again. It had been like old times—almost. He'd whispered some nonsense about how it was better this time because they were in a bed together for the first time—as if he was sentimental about such things—and then he'd told her he wasn't sure he knew how to make love to her without keeping one eye on the lookout and maybe he couldn't make love to her behind a closed door. There was no breeze blowing against his ass, and no sandy grit blowing in his eyes. Under these softer, more private and less primitive conditions, how could he make love to her?

She'd laughed, told him to shut up and get on with it.

He'd sunk into her, and she'd closed her eyes in ecstasy, realizing all his teasing had just been a way to keep the moment light. But it hadn't been light—it had been heavy, intense, earth-shattering.

She couldn't send him away.

"I think we all agreed it's safest. They're going to come for him."

"We don't know that." She turned to face her brothers as they ganged up on her in the kitchen. They were stuffing their faces with Fiona's good pancakes, grits and eggs, slurping coffee, generally plowing through enough food to feed a platoon. "Anyway, it doesn't matter. He wouldn't leave if I told him to."

It wasn't the whole truth. She'd mentioned witness

protection to Xav—then he'd pulled the tiny red thong off with his teeth, finding something to occupy himself with that made her gasp with sheer pleasure, the conversation had ended. It didn't come up again.

They'd made love, and when the babies awakened for their feeding, they'd made an assembly line of feeding, diapering, burping, comforting. She'd thought she was too exhausted after that to make love again, but Xav surprised her, gently loving her, telling her to relax in his arms, that he'd take care of her.

He had, and she was still smiling this morning.

"You'll have to tell him," Tighe said. "This is not his battle."

"He's a new father," Jace said quietly. "He has to realize that sooner or later, the cartel will figure out what happened. He was the only person in Wild with you."

"Maybe they don't know that." Even as she said it, Ash knew that wasn't likely.

"Somebody took those bodies," Falcon said. "They didn't just get up and walk away on their own."

"Unless they weren't dead," Galen said, his voice hopeful.

"I should have killed him the first time." Ash heard the cold flatness in her voice, the soft, incandescent memories of last night in Xav's arms fleeing from her. It had been her responsibility to deal with Wolf—she'd been born for that moment.

"You know what you have to do," Sloan said after a long moment, and then her brothers faded out of the kitchen, heading off to do chores.

She sat on a stool, stared at the wreckage of empty plates and depleted coffeepots. It was still dark outside, 5:30 a.m. on a frosty cold morning. She'd left Xav sleeping, his big body hogging the bed, one arm thrown over her pillow where she'd pushed him off her, a leg dangling off the side of the bed. It was the first time they'd ever slept together, and she'd intended to tease him today that she'd tamed him.

She couldn't tease him now. Her brothers were right. She was living in a dreamworld.

She heard a sound, glanced toward the kitchen window. Wolf's face peered in at her, his eyes fixed on her, nightmarish in their intensity and hatred, and a scream ripped out of her, right out of her soul.

Chapter Seven

Something stabbed at Xav, warning him that something was terribly wrong with Ash.

He jumped out of bed and fumbled in the dark for his clothes. By the soft glow of the night-light, he saw his four babies snoozing, undisturbed and content. Taking a deep breath, he tried to tell himself he had just had a bad dream.

But the crazy wild adrenaline in his veins wouldn't subside. He grabbed his clothes, stuck his gun in the holster at his back. "Off we go to the main house. We're going to check on your mother, who should be in bed next to me, but isn't." He put his children in the big-wheeled stroller, felt guilty for taking them out in the bitter cold across the snow-covered grounds, but decided they were wrapped as well as enchiladas and with a heavy blanket over them, they'd never notice.

Skye's eyes opened when he moved her, and he could have sworn she looked right at him and knew exactly what he was doing. "It's okay, little angel. Go back to sleep. Nothing's going to happen to you. Daddy's going to make sure of that." He slipped her in next to her brothers and sister, and hauled ass with the stroller.

He could hear shouting and yells, realized the Callahans were already on the scene. Xav picked up his pace, fearful for the first time in his life.

"What the hell?" he demanded, lifting the stroller up over the kitchen stoop and wheeling the babies inside.

The place was a shambles. Ash was in the center of her brothers. Fiona furiously cleaned the kitchen and Burke hunched at a window with a shotgun in his lap, staring out. The hidden gun cabinet was unlocked and open for the first time he could ever remember. Also, the door to the secret elevator was open. "What's going on in here?"

He hurried to Ash, kissing her, taking her in his arms just as the babies set up a furious wailing, probably not happy that the stroller had quit rolling. Fiona and some Callahans hurried over to grab up babies, and Xav was amazed by how handy the big men were at comforting the little ones.

Lots of practice.

"What happened, babe?"

Ash stared up at him, almost blankly, as if she was in shock. "I saw Wolf. He was here."

"No." He held her close. "He wasn't, Ash. You saw something in the snow. Or had a—" He didn't want to say nightmare, she was awake, but maybe a vision? Was it possible?

"It was Wolf," Ash said. "I saw him."

He lifted her chin so he could look deep into her eyes. "Honey, Wolf is dead. So is Rhein."

"There were no bodies."

"Doesn't matter. They're never coming back." In spite of his brave words, he could see Ash was really shaken up. He could feel her trembling. Ash wasn't given to flights of fancy and imagination. If she said she saw something, she had—and whatever it was had scared the bejesus out of her. "I won't leave you again. I promise."

"I left you," she said. "I came to get both of us coffee. I wanted to visit with Fiona. Talking to her in the early morning is one of my favorite things." She indicated the broken mugs on the floor.

"No worries. Just sit here and rest." He started to clean up the mess but Fiona handed him Skye and said, "You just take care of your family."

She put two fresh mugs beside him and he smiled at Fiona gratefully. "Hey, beautiful," he said to Ash, "why don't you let me put you in bed for a nap?"

She shook her head. "I don't want to leave here."

He nodded. "Galen," he said, and Galen looked up. "Maybe you should do a doc check on your sister," he murmured. "She seems a little traumatized."

Galen took Ash's hand, leading her out of the kitchen into the den. Xav followed with Skye.

"Ash," he heard Galen say, "you're safe."

"I know," she said. "Galen, we're not winning."

"We are. We will," Galen said. "We're not beaten yet. You're just frightened, and that's understandable." He rubbed his sister's shoulders. "We only let him win when we allow him to make us afraid."

"I'm not afraid," Ash murmured.

"We know who we are," Galen said, his voice hypnotic and strange. Xav leaned close to hear better, and even little Skye appeared to listen intently. "We know why we're here, and we know we're strong. We're a family. No one comes in, and no one goes out without our choosing."

"Okay," Ash said, sounding tired all of a sudden but

no longer panicked. She allowed Galen to lay her on the sofa, putting her feet up. Galen moved his hand in front of her eyes, whispered, "Sleep now," and Ash's body appeared to give up its tension and relax.

She didn't move again.

"She'll rest now," Galen said, getting up. "She'll be fine."

Skye was asleep in Xav's arms, too. He looked at Galen.

"If she says Wolf was here, then he was," Galen said, and took Skye from him, placing the baby against her mother's side, tucked between Ash and the sofa cushion. Neither of them moved, as if a spell had been cast over them.

"How?" Xav asked. "How could he be here?"

"We'll know soon enough," Galen said, and departed.

Xav stared at his wife and daughter, promising himself that no matter what, he was never leaving Ash—or their family—ever.

Whatever evil was coming to Rancho Diablo was going to have to get through him.

"HERE," FIONA SAID, appearing beside him in the den three hours later, "I'll keep an eye on them. You go figure out your life."

Xav shook his head, followed her into the kitchen while Ash slept on, a sleeping beauty to his worried gaze. It was late morning, and he'd checked on Ash and Skye several times, both of them content in their peaceful sleep. Skye hadn't awakened yet for a feeding, though he'd been on watch for the call. The kitchen had cleared out, the brothers long gone, the gun cabinet locked, the coffeepot full and percolating again—as if nothing had happened. Late-morning light seemed to have chased away all the demons of the dark.

Yet the calmness was deceptive. "What should I be figuring out?"

Fiona gave him a shrewd look. "First of all, I'd say you need to head into town to find truck tires. Yours have been slashed."

The coffee mug he'd been holding didn't quite make it to his lips. "When did that happen?"

"While we were all inside this morning with Ash."

"So Ash did see someone. Maybe not Wolf, but someone."

"I don't know." Fiona brought a fragrant spice cake out of the oven, setting it on the counter to cool. "Could have been a vision."

"I don't believe in visions."

"Don't say that too loudly around here." Fiona smiled, studied her recipe. "I think brownies, too, don't you? Roast in the Crock-Pot for dinner, with green chili corn bread and perhaps a fruit compote."

She was paying him no attention. "Fiona, Ash didn't have a vision. There was no hobgoblin or ghost out there. I know everyone here believes in things that go boo in the night, but I don't. I'm a simple man, the son of a tough-as-nails man who built his own international company selling heavy equipment, and I'm telling you, Gil Phillips would no more have tolerated dreams and visions than talk of leprechauns. He thought Santa Claus was a radical retailing plot."

Fiona gasped. "Don't say that so loud! Skye is just in the other room! And the babies are in my room with Burke! Sound travels!"

"Sorry, sorry." He took the warm slice of cake she handed him, perching on a barstool and tucking in. "I'm just saying, someone was here, and it wasn't a ghost. Ash didn't have some kind of phantasmagoric nightmare. The problem at Rancho Diablo isn't superstitious folklore, it's criminals. We just have to solve that."

"Fancy talk coming from a suit," Fiona said, her gaze on him.

"Maybe, but the suit in me is practical. The way to run a business is to believe in numbers and facts. Statistics."

"You don't believe in magic?"

"I don't believe in anything I can't see, Fiona."

She sighed. "So if we look at everything through the lens of the hard-baked realist, what are you going to do now with your wife and four Christmas angels?" She gazed at him woefully. "I know Galen and the brothers and Ash think you should go into hiding, but I'm just old and selfish enough to not want you to. I *am* getting old," she said on a dramatic sigh, "I came to this country from Ireland to take care of six Callahan boys, my sister Molly's children, because she and her husband, Jeremiah, knew they'd stirred up a real hornet's next, and they opted not to separate the boys and put them through a life on the run. I know they were right, and I know Carlos and Julia were right for doing the same and leaving their family in the tribe, but now, I'm hoping your path can be different. I just don't want to give up Skye and Thorn and Briar and Valor. Or anyone anymore," Fiona said, and padded off down the hall, her usual whirlwind gait lacking and slow.

Xav stared after her. He felt her life force tiring, the weight and strain of the years of standing in the face of danger protecting the Callahan creed and clan wearing her down. He didn't believe in magic and spiritual things, but he did believe people's hearts and minds created the magic of life, and Fiona had done that for the Callahan family.

He would do it for his now. He remembered the strange sensation of warning, a sixth sense kicking in this morning that something was dreadfully wrong with Ash, that had sent him running to find her. If his wife-to-be, whom he loved more than the breath of life itself, wanted to stay here, he was staying, too—no matter how hard she tried to run him off.

Besides, he'd never been much good at running away. He had too much Gil Phillips in him for that.

"THERE WAS NO Christmas ball this year," Fiona announced to Ash after she'd awakened. She sat up, staring at her tiny aunt perched on the chair across from her, holding baby Skye in her arms. "No Christmas ball, so don't fear that you missed anything. I had no holiday spirit without you, and I hope you don't go away again."

Ash pushed her sluggish brain back into focus. "How long was I asleep?"

"Well, let's see," Fiona said cheerfully. "It was about six this morning, or earlier, when you gave me a fright I won't soon forget. You shrieked like a banshee, and we all came running. It's now five in the afternoon, so you must have really needed your rest. And thankfully for the babies, there was plenty of breast milk in the freezer."

"I need to go take care of that," she said, feeling heavy and sore. But the sleep had been fabulous. She remembered Wolf's face staring in at her and suppressed a shiver. "Where is everybody?"

"Running thither and yon as usual." Fiona looked at her. "I will say you're more beautiful than when you left Rancho Diablo, niece. Although I wish you hadn't gone in the first place."

"I didn't want to go." Ash stood, went to hug Fiona. "I wish you'd had your annual Christmas ball."

"There's always next year. I'm just getting old and sentimental, I'm afraid."

"You're darling, and I love you."

Fiona cleared her throat. "Are you in love with Xav?"

Ash blinked. "I have been for years."

"Then you should try on the magic wedding dress," Fiona said softly. "It's been waiting all these years for you."

Ash laughed. "Fiona, dresses don't wait. They're not alive. You and that dress!" she said, laughing again. "Sometimes I think you believe it really is magic."

"What does one believe in, I ask you, if not magic? Fairy tales? The supernatural?" Fiona looked offended. "Even when I go to church, I feel the Holy Spirit. The unexplainable is a good thing."

"No, no," Ash said hurriedly, "I didn't mean to offend you, Auntie. I know the magic wedding dress is very special. I'm thrilled you want me to try it on."

"But?" Fiona demanded. "I hear a but."

"I'm just not ready. I'm all spooked and wrinkled up from seeing Wolf this morning."

"Ash, that wasn't Wolf you saw," Fiona said. "Honey, you had a daymare."

"I don't think so." Yet she didn't want to frighten Fiona, either, so she said, "I'm going to check on the babies, pump some breast milk and shower up. Then," she said, dropping a kiss on Fiona's cheek and one on Skye's, "if you really want me to, I'll try on the dress. Just for grins, not because I'm getting married. But if it'll make you happy, we'll both satisfy our curiosity on what I'd look like in a wedding dress. I'm not the lacy-dress kind of girl, as everyone knows," Ash said, "but it'll be a bonding moment for you and me."

Fiona beamed. "If you only knew how long I've waited for this, Ashlyn. All the other brides married into the family, but you're the only Callahan who will have ever tried on the dress. Not even Julia and Molly got to, of course, nor did I. The magic reminds me that happy endings are still possible. Even here."

She took Skye and left the den, a delighted smile on her face. Ash went to find her other children and her husband, unable to completely put away the terror she'd felt at seeing Wolf's face at the window.

It had been no daymare.

Chapter Eight

Running Bear approached Xav at the stone-and-fire ring in the canyons as Xav stared out across the sandy, winding arroyo that led to the other ranch, which the brothers called Loco Diablo and which Ash called Sister Wind Ranch.

Galen had said all the land had been parceled out, but the cartel and Wolf's mercenaries had tunneled underneath Loco Diablo, putting in an underground of well-fortressed mazes. The land had become Wolf's staging area, with plans for the networked tunnels to reach the Callahans' ranch. Years had been dedicated to the goal of taking Rancho Diablo from below—until they'd been discovered.

Loco Diablo might not ever be inhabitable now, not by law-abiding folks just wanting to work the land and raise cattle or crops. Ash said they should just pour concrete over the land and put in schools, a hospital, other things that could benefit the community. She said this was a way to heal the damage to the land and the negative energy that had been sown into the soil by Wolf and his men.

Xav thought her idea was excellent.

"Xav," Running Bear said, finally situating himself on the ground and deciding to speak.

Xav sat near him. "Hello, Chief."

"Thank you for bringing Ashlyn home."

He looked pleased, and Xav hoped that meant he'd done the right thing by bringing Ash and the children here. "I was happy to do it."

"You have four children."

"Have you been by to see them?"

Running Bear shook his head. "I will go soon."

"Good. That'll make Ash happy."

"Wolf is not dead."

Xav stared at the chief, whose wrinkled, dark-skinned face was devoid of expression, his dark eyes completely convinced of what he was saying. "I don't understand. I shot those two men."

"Rhein is dead. Wolf is not."

It was the worst possible news. Xav couldn't believe it. "I did my best."

"I know. It was not meant to be."

He looked toward Loco Diablo, across the wide canyon that stretched dark rose and dusty against the backdrop of a turquoise sky. "How is it meant to be?"

"We will know soon."

That didn't give him much to go on. "Is Ash safe?"

Running Bear turned to him. "No one is safe."

"You're going to say I should take her and the children and go."

"I do not know what you are called to do. You are not a Callahan. Your path is not for me to know."

"And Ash?" His heart sank. "What is her path?"

"Her path is her path." Running Bear seemed content with his assessment. "Only Ash will know what the spirits guide her to do."

"I don't believe in that," Xav said. "I believe we make a plan, we follow it and we flush these criminals out of here. Cover all of Loco Diablo with concrete and put in a theme park and a rodeo, I don't care. But put them out of business once and for all."

Running Bear nodded, and it seemed as if his onyx eyes smiled a little, but Xav wouldn't have sworn to it. "You are impatient."

"Damn right I am." He took a deep breath. "Okay, I'm not a Callahan. I freely admit that I don't have the propensity for outthinking the enemy. In my father's world, in the world I know best—" He thought about that for a moment. "Hell, my father just ironed his enemies flat. Rolled over them like they were paper."

"And you want to do that."

"Yes, I do." Action instead of defense. Ash's fright this morning had him worried. Whether she would admit it or not, Ash had been terrified by Wolf's appearance. If Running Bear was right and Wolf was alive, then Wolf was on the ranch, close enough to attack.

"I've got to go, Chief. I need to get home."

Running Bear didn't say anything. He looked toward the sky at a hawk circling above.

"Come by and see the babies. They'd like to meet their great-grandfather."

Running Bear didn't answer, and Xav knew he was no longer thinking about him, or Ash, or the Callahans. His mind was on the hawk and whatever else only Running Bear understood.

Xav galloped back to the ranch, checking for cell service, his heart burning with sudden fear that something was very wrong at Rancho Diablo.

ASH WENT UP THE STAIRS SLOWLY, not really certain it was necessary to don the fabled gown but wanting to please Fiona more than anything. It was hard to deny the sweet-natured aunt such a simple request.

She'd try the dress on, then tell Fiona thank you for the thoughtful gesture—but she'd also tell her the truth: there were no sparks, no glitter bouncing around the attic, and no handsome man revealing himself to be her one true love, as the Callahan brides had all claimed would happen.

She already knew who her one true love was, had known for years. She wasn't going to marry Xav, so magic wedding dress or no, there'd be no charmed fairy-tale ending. She couldn't put her finger on what was wrong, she just knew something was, and marrying Xav wasn't going to stop the evil she felt following her, encompassing her.

But a more sinister thought occurred to her. What if it wasn't Xav whose handsome face she saw? Ash shivered. She didn't dare put on the dress, even as nonsensical as she thought Fiona's wedding tales were. There was no point in tempting the spirits.

"Hey!" Xav yelled up the attic stairs. "Ash!"

Startled, Ash squealed, peered down the stairs. "You bellowed loud enough to wake the dead!"

He stared up at her. "Hey, beautiful."

"Do you have to yell when you want to get my attention?" she demanded, miffed even though the sight of Xav grinning up the stairs at her was enough to wipe away most of her ire.

"The spirit moved me to call loudly, just in case you weren't thinking about me," he said, "except I know that's impossible. I know my girl, and I'm always on her mind. Hey, what are you doing up there? Looking for Christmas decorations?"

"Maybe. Can you go away?"

"I could, but I'd rather come up there and help you. I don't want you carrying boxes down by yourself. Let your big, strong, handsome husband help you. Besides which, we need to talk, and the attic is a nice, quiet place for us to have this conversation."

"I'm busy."

He headed up the stairs anyway because he simply had no concept of not being wanted, probably because Xav knew she did want him.

She shook her head as he cleared the landing. "I noticed you referenced yourself as my husband. In case you're living in an alternate universe where weddings take place just because you think they should, we're not married."

"I'm married in my heart. So we're married." He shrugged, a rebel with a dead-sexy smile. "If everybody else around here can go on dreams and mumbo jumbo, so can this cowboy."

He leaned over and kissed her, smooching her until she felt her toes literally curl in her black suede boots. "Not here in the attic, Xav," Ash said breathlessly. "Someone might come upstairs."

He looked at her. "Is this the same woman who chased me from canyon to canyon and made love to me in every conceivable crevice and cave in front of the angels and the constellations, without the slightest bit of worry for anything except getting next to my big, strong body?"

"You don't think much of yourself, do you?"

"It just so happens that I do. And you do, too. Come

on, gorgeous, let's make a little—" He glanced around the attic, his gaze curious. "There are no Christmas decorations up here. I see a mirror, a closet, a sofa, some antique chairs, but no festive decorations."

She raised her brows, said nothing.

"What are you doing up here, little lady?" Xav asked.

"Hiding from you," she said sweetly.

"Well, that won't work. There's no place on earth that I can't find you, as you should know by now."

That did seem to be true, or she wouldn't be at Rancho Diablo. "What do you want, anyway?"

"Don't remind me about why I'm here right now. I'm in full avoidance mode, especially if you're offering kisses," he said, glancing around the attic again. His gaze caught on the closet. "Is that where the fairy-tale gown is stashed?" he asked, his voice quiet, as if he didn't want anyone to overhear.

"Why are you whispering?"

"Seems like the right thing to do up here. I'm going to open the closet and find out."

"No!"

He looked at her with a teasing grin. "Oh, babe. I know what's going on. You came up here to try on Fiona's magic muumuu, didn't you?"

"Muumuu? Really?"

He scooped her into his arms. "Babe, you're wild about me, and your mind is on settling me. Hence you sneaking up here for a preview of the supposedly supernatural garment. Admit it."

"Put me down and go away."

"I can't believe it. This is awesome!" He gave her a huge kiss that made her suddenly wonder if Fiona's attic might be just the place for a sexy rendezvous after all. "Ash Callahan, you came up here to experience the Callahan magic for yourself—which can only mean one thing."

"And that would be what?"

"You're *seriously* contemplating taking the wedding walk with me."

"I'm seriously not."

He kissed her. "Sweetheart, I know you too well, and right now, I can tell you are fibbing your cute little heart out." He sat down on the sofa with an exaggerated *oof* and smiled into her eyes as he situated her in his lap. "You go right ahead and drag out the wonderful wedding rig. I'm itching to see it on you." He sighed with happiness and pushed her off. "Go on. I'm looking forward to the show."

"I'm not going to do it." Not in front of him, she wasn't. He was *so* sure that she would fall into his arms like an overripe plum—the way she always had. The way she wanted to right this minute.

"You were going to before I found you," he stated, sure of himself.

"Even if you're right, I'm not now."

"You're so adorable when you're shy."

"I'm not the least bit shy."

He got up, strode to the closet. "I'll get you started. I'm dying to see this thing on you." He stopped, turned to look at her, his hand still on the doorknob. "You realize the Callahan wives tell stories about seeing their one true love when they put on the gown?"

"Yes," she said, distinctly unwilling to discuss this angle.

"It's preposterous."

"Of course it is."

He grinned at her. "I get it. You're scared you won't see me!"

She shrugged. "This conversation is silly, the premise absurd."

"But let's visit Fiona World for a second," he said, "wouldn't it be a downer if you didn't see me?"

"Why would it be a downer?" she demanded.

"Because we have four children. So I'm the only man you're ever going to have," he said, obviously quite sure of this. "It would be just too bad if you didn't see me in a princely vision."

She shook her head. "This conversation is so ridiculous. Xav, let's just go downstairs."

He grinned at her. "Fiona knows you're up here, doesn't she?"

"Of course!"

"Aha! There are wedding plans afoot!" He looked very pleased about that. "Don't be embarrassed about wanting me, angel."

She smiled. "*Embarrassed* isn't the word that comes to mind. *Annoyed,* maybe."

He stroked the inside of her arm, staring at her intently. "I want the best for you."

"And you're the best?"

"Yes. Of course." A shadow crossed his face. "I am the best thing for you. In fact, I just had a long talk with Running Bear, which is how I know I'm the only man for you." He put his arms around her, and she leaned into him, enjoying his strong, stubborn warmth, before she remembered she shouldn't give in to him quite as easily as she always seemed to. "Some things aren't what they seem," Xav said.

"I'm a Callahan. I think I know that."

"Some things are worse than they seem."

An uneasy tickle swept her. "What are you talking about?"

"Sh—" he said. "Walls have ears."

"Not up here they don't." She frowned, having the strangest feeling that something was really bugging him.

"They might," he said. "One never knows with the Callahans." He got up, kissed her hand and disappeared down the stairs.

"Great. There goes my prince." She glanced toward the closet. "You're just going to have to wait. My man is having a brain fart of some epic variety."

She thought she saw a tiny twinkle burst through a crack between the doorway and the frame of the closet, but of course it was probably just a piece of dust filtering in the light. Ash shook her head at the fantastical imaginings Fiona's tales had put in her mind and headed downstairs.

"What did you want to tell me?" Ash asked when she found him in the kitchen pouring two cups of coffee.

He looked so serious he scared her. Ash felt herself get a bit dizzy from fear washing over her.

"Where are the babies?" she demanded. "Are they all right?"

"They're fine," he said quickly. "They're with Fiona and Burke, and I think some of Fiona's friends are visiting, spoiling the babies to death. Mavis, Nadine and Corinne."

"Her Books'n'Bingo Society friends," Ash murmured.

"That's what Fiona said. Anyway, as I mentioned,

I ran into Running Bear at the stone-and-fire ring today—"

She looked at him. "No one *runs* into Running Bear. He's never anywhere by accident." Particularly not at the stone-and-fire ring. When she and her brothers had come to Rancho Diablo many years ago, Running Bear had instructed them to meet at the stone-and-fire circle. They'd been separated for years, not seeing each other as they went through life in the military and then on their own—and suddenly, they'd all received secret messages from Grandfather to meet at the location he specified, in a place called Rancho Diablo in New Mexico. The circle had seven stones, one for each of them, with a small fire lit in the center. Running Bear tended the fire, though he never said so. That strange and amazing day, when Grandfather had brought their family back together, he'd told them that the circle was their new home, their touchstone for remaining a family, while they served this urgent mission. No matter what happened at Rancho Diablo, they always had a home.

They'd agreed to protect Rancho Diablo and keep the land safe from the cartel, allowing their Callahan cousins to stay far away in Hell's Colony with their many children. The Chacon Callahans had been raised in the tribe, each of them training in the military when they were old enough. They were uniquely qualified to take on the mission. "What was on Grandfather's mind?"

Xav pulled her to him, held her close. "Babe, that vision you saw this morning was no vision. Wolf is alive."

Chapter Nine

Xav watched as the woman he loved went to the hidden gun closet, unlocked it and pulled out a 9 mm handgun. "What are you doing, angel?"

"Apparently I left some unfinished business in Texas. I'm going to go take care of it."

"Whoa, hang on, sweetheart." He went to her, took the gun away and put it back into the cabinet. He wanted to kiss away the frown suddenly creasing her face. "Killing a man in premeditated cold blood's not going to do our children any good."

"You tried to," Ash said.

"That wasn't premeditated. You were being kidnapped. Of course I wasn't going to allow that. And anyway, that was then and this is now. You and I are going to have cool heads and think this through. We have four amazing children counting on us to do the right thing."

"The right thing is killing Wolf." She looked at him. "This is impossible! I know they were both dead, Wolf and Rhein. I *know* they were, Xav."

"Rhein is dead," Xav said quietly. "Which is no doubt going to make Wolf even more eager for revenge."

"Well, tough crackers. I want revenge, too. Only one of us is going to get it."

He had to convince her to focus more on mothering, and frankly, marrying him, than being a warrior. "Can you trust me to take care of this? And you take care of our children? One of us needs to be with them around the clock. Fiona and Burke aren't really strong enough to withstand an attack, and I wouldn't want them to have to. Let me and your brothers handle this, babe, and you keep the babies safe."

"It's not your fight."

His sassy lady. "I love you madly, Ash." He kissed her deeply, enjoying every second their lips touched. "But if I have to lock you in your room, I will."

She shrugged. "Wouldn't do a bit of good."

He didn't doubt that for a second. "Let's put our heads together and come up with a plan of attack, if you insist on being part of the action."

"You watch the children because you'd be a far better bodyguard, and I'll go kill my uncle, which I should have done in the first place."

He pulled his darling, revenge-thirsty wife into his arms. "You shouldn't kill him, because your grandfather said not to, and Running Bear knows best."

"This is true," she murmured reluctantly.

"All right, then. We let fate take care of Wolf."

"Fate has been stinking at her job lately."

"Not altogether. She brought the two of us together at long last. Right?" He desperately wanted to make love to his wife, reassure her that everything was going to be just fine.

Unfortunately, at this point, he wasn't sure that was a promise anyone would believe.

"Fate didn't bring us together. What brought us together was the fact that I chased you for a good solid several years, and—"

"And I won you at last year's Christmas ball auction," Xav said.

Ash's eyes went wide. "You're the one who put up the winning bid? Everyone said I put up my own bid anonymously so I wouldn't have to go out with anyone yucky. Blind dates are no fun, so apparently I bought my way out."

He laughed. "It was so much fun hearing that tale. I encouraged it, you know."

"Did you?"

"Yes. I didn't want you to know it was me."

She eyed him, her gaze softening, which he thought was a hopeful sign. "Why didn't you ever collect?"

"Because the time wasn't right. But I'm collecting now," he said, kissing her, holding her tight.

She melted against him, which felt better than anything he'd ever been able to conjure in his dreams when they'd been apart those long many months. "You're just trying to get my mind off of Wolf."

"Yes, I am. Does no good to think about him. There's nothing he can do to hurt us or our family."

"What did Running Bear say?"

He kissed her forehead. "You know Running Bear. He isn't exactly loose with information."

"I can't believe Wolf is still alive. I thought we were free," Ash murmured. She looked up at him. "Next you're going to tell me we have to go into witness protection. Or hiding."

He stared down at the woman he loved more than

anything. "Actually, I hadn't thought that far ahead. I figured you and I would map out a game plan."

"That's very democratic of you. No demands, no carrying me over your shoulder caveman-style?"

"Not unless you want me to, in which case I could be easily talked into a caveman impersonation."

"I don't feel like it, I guess," she said, sort of sagging against his chest, and Xav winced.

He stroked her long silvery ponytail. "It's going to be all right, babe. I don't know how. I just know it will be."

WHEN SHE'D FIRST HEARD Wolf hadn't been sent to Hell where he belonged, Ash's first reaction was to go send him there herself.

Her second reaction was to shore up the defenses where the babies were concerned. She moved the babies from the outlying bunkhouse to the main house, where there were always people coming in and out. "We're hiding in plain sight," she told the babies. "There's probably no place safer than being surrounded by family, this family." Here at Rancho Diablo they would learn their heritage, too, which would make them strong. She could go to Xav's family compound in Hell's Colony for protection, where her children would be guarded by the Callahan cousins, but her family was here. Whatever happened, she wanted to be with them.

She wanted to be with Xav.

"We're not afraid, anyway," she murmured to Skye as she nursed her, then diapered her and put her gently back in the bassinet. "Life isn't about fear. It's about strength."

Skye's blue, blue gaze stared back at her. "I love you," she murmured to her daughter. "I can see my soul, and Running Bear's soul, when I look in your eyes. And I think you already possess the wisdom. You're my special angel." She touched Skye's hand, and Skye curled her fingers around hers. Love burst inside Ash. "I won't let anything happen to you."

She kissed her and picked up Thorn for his turn. If Skye was part of her soul, Thorn was her impatient baby. "You have your father's desire for action," she told Thorn, nursing him. "You want everything to happen now."

Thorn's navy eyes looked up at her as he nursed. She smiled, touched his face. "You're going to break some hearts."

Twenty minutes later, he was drowsy and ready for his bassinet. She went down to the kitchen and got some breast milk, hurried back up the stairs as she heard Valor give a wail that clearly denoted his anxiety that his meal wasn't coming as fast as his siblings'. "I'm not leaving you out," she whispered to Valor. "I'm just a little tired today, so be patient." She kissed him and put the bottle in his mouth, and he slowly relaxed when he realized he wasn't going to get left out of dinner.

She stroked his cheek, wondering why she was so tired, drawn. Usually she could nurse all the babies, but not this afternoon—and she realized the news that Wolf was alive had shocked her deeply.

She looked at her babies, wondered what the future held for them, wondered if her mother had thought the same thing, felt the same unease and wistful longing for a peaceful, spiritual home to raise her family.

It's going to be different this time. Right here, right now, Wolf no longer affects this family.

"Hey," Xav said, walking into the room. "Leave a

forwarding address the next time you decide to move us, okay?"

"You said you could find me anywhere."

"This is true," he said, touching his son's head, stroking the tiny tuft of hair. "But it would be nice not to have a heart attack when I walk into the bunkhouse and find it empty."

"You managed."

"Fiona pointed me in the right direction. She said you'd commandeered some of your brothers to move baby gear." He glanced around. "So we're living in the big house now."

"We." She gave him an arch look.

He leaned down to kiss her. "There's no way I'm not sticking to you like glue after the drama with Wolf. But if you're worried about your reputation or you're a little squeamish on living with a man before marriage, I suggest you call the deacon and fix it."

He kissed her again, just to let her know she couldn't resist him, then picked up little Briar, who was waiting patiently for her meal. "I'll feed this one," he said. "You're not last, sweetie. You were just waiting for Daddy, weren't you?" he murmured to his daughter.

Ash watched, astonished, as Xav chose one of the bottles she'd prepared. He slung a towel over his shoulder, put the baby against his chest, and slipped the bottle in her mouth as if he'd done it a thousand times.

"That's right," he told his daughter. "Daddy's little girl is glad to see him."

Ash's heart seemed to fall an inch inside her. "If I marry you, will you stop being Mr. Perfect? I'm feeling anything but Miss Perfect."

"You were never perfect, darling," Xav said, looking over at her. "What I like about you is how imperfect you are."

"Is that so?"

"Yes. Your flaws make you interesting."

"My flaws?"

"Yeah. Like when you're argumentative."

"You mean when you're trying to get your way, and I don't go along with it immediately?"

"Like now," he said, winking. "And like you not wanting to get married. It's all very sexy."

"Not getting married is for your own good."

"I don't believe in that 'hunted one' gobbledygook," Xav said. "So if you're trying to convince me that you're saving me by not marrying me, saving me from a fate worse than death or whatever, I say don't underestimate me, cupcake. I can take a little Callahan chaos."

"It would serve you right if I did marry you."

"Yes," Xav said, undaunted. "I have my children to think of. It's important to set good examples for the kiddies."

"They're a little young, don't you think, to be worried about examples?"

"My parents were married." He shrugged. "My old man was a tough ol' son of a gun, as you know. Mom put up with his foibles and cranks, and she's tough, too. They stayed together through thick and thin. *Together*."

"I met her once," Ash said, "when I went out to the compound."

"Mom only served us vegetarian meals. She said it was to keep the old man healthy, and it was her way of keeping us all healthy. It didn't work in the end for Pop because he was just too mean. He checked out of life early." Xav got up, put Briar into her bassinet with a tender smile. "Now she's off sailing the world with her new man. But the rest of us, we still know that our family made us what we are today. Kendall, Shaman, Gage and me, we're a family because of those two characters."

Ash smiled as he took Valor from her, put him into his bassinet, too. "So you and I are going to be characters whom our children look back on as being the hot steel that forge their characters?"

"We're going to be a family," he said, pulling her into his lap. "You have no argument, lady. Remember when you told me that because I'd killed Wolf, you'd brought the Callahan curse on me?"

"I do indeed remember," she said, a little breathlessly as he kissed her neck.

"As much as I was thrilled that I'd taken him out of the picture, it turns out I didn't. So I'm not cursed by anything Callahan, unless you consider me not killing him a curse, which I do. I only bring all this up so that you will know you have absolutely zero reason not to marry me, gorgeous."

Maybe it wasn't true—maybe she wasn't the hunted one. Perhaps the curse was more of a challenge, something to be avoided by hunkering down and staying together as a family until Wolf and the cartel finally went away, once they realized this family couldn't be broken. None of them, Callahan or Chacon Callahan.

"You're probably right," she said, because she wanted to believe it. "But Wolf is still here, and I suppose none of us are really safe."

"I'm going out now," Xav said. "You take a nap, get some rest for the twenty minutes these gentle spoiled angels of ours sleep. The next time I see you, I want you to be ready to discuss marriage. Because I know you were upstairs trying to sneak a peek at the magic wedding dress for a reason." He smiled, brushed her lips with his, and left.

She waited. He popped his head back inside the room.

"Deal?" Xav asked.

Everything inside her wanted to say yes. It made sense what he said. Nothing had happened to him because of her, and none of them had killed Wolf after all, which meant that they'd kept to the law and letter of Running Bear's command.

There was no reason not to say yes, especially with all the good arguments he gave. They were already parents, and they did need to set good examples for the children. They'd be stronger together.

She smiled. "Go away."

"That's my girl. Always sweet and delicate."

He disappeared, and she could hear him whistling lightly, a content tune that made him sound like a man without a care in the world. She pushed away the worry and headed to grab a quick shower.

If she wasn't the hunted one Running Bear had always spoken of, then who was?

"Our first Christmas all together," Fiona said, delighted, as she decorated the tree. She'd had new ornaments painted for Valor, Skye, Briar and Thorn with their names and birth dates on them, and she placed them on the tree with glee. "Every last Callahan married," she said with relish. "Married with children, better still."

Ash situated the babies near the tree on a plush down pallet so they could lay together. She put a soft mobile over their heads, which caught their attention, even though they probably couldn't make out very much of what they were seeing. Still, they seemed watchful.

"I'm not married," she reminded her aunt.

"Yet," Fiona said, unbothered. "But it's only a matter of time. I heard Xav tell Running Bear that if he can drag you to the altar, he hopes your grandfather will agree to give you away. Every girl should have someone give her away—it's tradition. And Xav is very traditional." Fiona smiled with satisfaction. "I thought it was sweet of him to ask Running Bear to stand in as your father figure."

A little dart of pain lodged inside Ash. She'd concentrated so much on not ever getting married that she'd never allowed herself to think about the sentiment; it was going to hurt that her father wasn't here to give her away. Still, she wasn't the world's most traditional woman, and tradition shouldn't matter so much, should it?

It mattered to her. Xav would one day proudly give away her daughters.

And Fiona was right: it was very princely of Xav to think of what would make their wedding special for her. "Blast," Ash said, "I asked him to stop being such a Prince Charming."

Fiona laughed. "Why?"

"Because it's hard to live up to."

"You're in love."

Fiona sounded sure, and Ash saw no reason to lie. "I have been for so long."

"Then it's time you quit worrying about the past and look to the future," Fiona said, placing a huge, sparkly gold star atop the tree.

"Maybe you're right." Why should she let Wolf spoil their lives any more than he already had? Her spirit strengthened as she looked down at her children. "You're right. What was I thinking?"

"That you were protecting your family. Of course you were." Fiona nodded decisively. "But we're not giving an inch more to the cartel than we have to."

Ash turned. "I haven't asked what's been happening with the cartel and the land across the canyons."

"Well, they cause their fair share of trouble. I thought I was doing the right thing by having Galen buy that land apart from the ownership of Rancho Diablo. I wanted all of you to work for it, get married, have families to win it. Back then, the lure seemed like a win/win scenario that would benefit all of you. It was all I wanted," Fiona said, sighing. "The thing is, that land's so torn up with tunnels running under it that even the feds are pretty lost as to how to stop it. All we have over there now is law enforcement scratching their heads. Wolf and his mercenaries are pretty dug in."

"Why did you send Xav to bring me home?"

"Because it's Christmas!" Fiona looked astonished. "I missed you."

"Fiona, you *knew,*" Ash said suddenly, realizing that the delicate painted china ornaments for the babies would have taken weeks to make. "You talked to Mallory, didn't you?"

Fiona looked a bit sheepish. "She might have called here once or twice. On disposable, untraceable phones."

"I was never really alone, was I?" Ash asked, and the memory of the moments of despair she'd felt were washed away by her family's love. "It was my journey, wasn't it? I just didn't recognize it."

"We all have a journey," Fiona said. "We support each other, we love each other when our journey comes to us. Mine was to come here," she said softly, her gaze turning toward the snow-laden landscape outside. "Sometimes I miss the green of Ireland, the hills, the beauty. But there was a battle there, too, that my parents fought. So I knew that life wasn't always easy. I came here when I was called, and Burke came with me. He never once said he didn't want to walk this path with me. He's the light of my life," she said, her smile soft, her aura serene and untroubled. "He understood the price we pay for freedom. No one lives without paying something for their decisions."

She turned to Ash. "You were never alone. Your children will never be alone. We will always be strong, no matter what comes."

"We haven't won yet," Ash said. "And sometimes I think it may be impossible."

"Do you?" Fiona asked. "Do you really think that when you look at your children?"

No. She didn't think the war was lost at all when she looked at Thorn, Skye, Valor, Briar. She'd never dreamed she'd have children. And then one day, they were suddenly a miraculous part of her life.

She couldn't imagine ever living without them. They blessed her in so many ways, changed her for the better.

"I love you, Aunt Fiona. Thank you for coming here. I know you miss your homeland, your friends, your way of life. Everything here is so very different from Ireland."

"The sacrifice is always worth it. In Ireland I didn't have children. Here I have more children than I could have ever imagined. Life is short, and what matters more than family and good friends?"

Ash stared at Fiona, seeing her aunt's strength in a

new way. Fiona had always been strong, but Ash had never really thought of her in terms of being a fighter. Now she realized just how much of a warrior Fiona was in her own soft, gentle way.

"You've carried the torch for our family."

"Actually, you allowed me to have exactly what I really wanted. The land never changes, not really. Mountains shift ever so slightly over time, but here is stability. Nothing can change that, not even Wolf's evil. And the land that I wanted you and your brothers to compete for was yours always." Fiona shrugged. "It was actually time more than land I was trying to give you. While you were here fighting for the truth, I didn't want your lives to slip away," she said with satisfaction. "Maybe I told a few fairy tales along the way to get you to go the right way, but I believe in happy endings."

Ash blinked. "You knew this would be a long journey, so you set up a competition so we'd all focus on the prize of the land, instead of just our assignment?"

"You were twenty-five when you came here. Now you're thirty, almost more. How many more years will be needed to be victorious I can't say. You could be thirty-five, your brothers older. I wouldn't take the gift of time from you, and that was all I had to give."

Ash thought about her beautiful children. "Thank you, Fiona, for being wiser than all of us."

She hugged her. "As I said, I got the ultimate prize. I got you. All the family I've been given is more to me than land or money. And one day, I know we will all be together. That thought keeps me going on this journey. My advice? Marry Xav sooner than later, and start a new journey with your family."

She flitted out of the den, leaving Ash beside her

children. Their gazes were no longer on the pretty mobile, but on the beautiful Christmas tree and the lovely twinkling lights Fiona had turned on. At the top of the tree, the star glittered, its beauty a beacon to the holidays.

"I was never alone," she told her children, "and now I know you babies never will be alone, either. Not for one step of the journeys each of you will take."

And somehow that thought gave her the courage she'd been missing for some time. She missed her parents, and she knew her brothers did, too. Somewhere in the mists of her mind were shadowy memories she could barely recall, of softness and joy, and the comfort of loving embraces. She hadn't been old enough to know them well when they'd had to leave. Maybe the memories she had were really mist and not real, just recollections of the fragmented pieces her brothers shared of their own memories. She wasn't sure. But somewhere back in the pieces of happy times she'd held so carefully, she knew she'd been loved, always had been.

"You'll always be loved," she told the babies suddenly. "No one can ever take that away from you. Even if I'm no longer here, you'll hold my spirit inside you."

And that was her only gift to her children right now, all that she had to give. She was a warrior, she was called to serve, and though she hadn't realized it until now, so were her unexpected and precious babies.

Fiona was right.

Everyone had their journey. The strong faced theirs and walked through the fire regardless of the sacrifices.

She no longer feared that journey. Her children had her gifts, as well as Xav's commitment and strength.

Whether she'd ever known it or not, she and Xav were two halves of the same person.

And she loved him even more for it.

She remembered her reluctance to try on the magic wedding dress. What was holding her back?

Even if her sisters-in-law swore that wonderful things happened because of the gown, Ash now knew those stories were tales of fancy from the lips of women who'd been head over heels in love. She smiled, thinking it had been silly to be afraid of marrying Xav. Why had she been so fearful?

The darkness inside her made her feel afraid. But Xav wasn't afraid of her darkness—he said he was a tough guy and a fearless badass. He laughed away *her* fears.

Maybe she'd just go catch her a badass husband, then. It was time to put her fears away and experience the magic for herself.

Chapter Ten

"When are you going to tell her?" Xav asked Running Bear, when the chief appeared beside him atop the snow-covered mesa. The days were shorter, the nights darker and colder. Something sinister stirred inside Xav, a pressing warning he could feel sitting heavy between his shoulders. Ash appeared more content than she'd ever been, her time spent almost exclusively with the babies now. But he kept a secret from her, and it troubled him. He'd waited for Running Bear to visit the ranch, but he hadn't yet been to see his great-grandchildren, a fact that puzzled Xav.

So he'd kept on ice the knowledge that had hit him one day, not about to share his realization, not even with Ash. In spirit, she seemed as though she was in waiting, hanging in some strange still place he'd never seen her inhabit before. She didn't mention Wolf anymore or her desire to kill him. It was almost as if she'd wiped Wolf and the danger around them out of her mind.

It unsettled Xav. He loved that she wanted to be with her children every minute, but he also worried that a little of her light had gone out, as if she turned a blind eye to the danger.

"I will not tell her," Running Bear said. "And though you know the truth, you will not tell Ash, either."

"Or any of the Callahans, I presume."

"It is not yet time."

Xav blew out a heavy breath, not feeling good about this. "Not that I'm doubting you, but don't you think it would be fairer to the Callahans if they knew about their parents?"

"If it was so easy to set the truth free, it would be done every day. We walk in the shadows when there is pain for other people by knowing the truth."

"I guess I can appreciate that." Still, Xav was troubled. "I'll play it your way."

"I know." Running Bear looked across the canyons toward Loco Diablo. "My son Wolf is in a killing rage."

A shaft of hatred sliced through Xav. "What do you want me to do about it? I assume you've shown up here for a reason."

"I want you to go to Wolf."

"Why?" Nothing could have shocked Xav more. "Trust me, you don't want me to do that. I already tried to kill him once, and I'm pissed that I failed. Frankly, my second shot will be everything I've got and then some."

Running Bear shook his head. "That is not your destiny."

"I'm not really a big believer in destiny. In my family, we do action. Bending people to our will, negotiating, stuff like that. I'm pretty sure my old man wasn't above greasing a palm or two to make his business successful internationally, and I'm sure I own those genes, too."

"Tell my son," Running Bear said, "that he is walking the wrong path. His destiny will soon be upon him if he does what he is planning."

Running Bear whistled and a Diablo galloped at full stride to the mesa from seemingly thin air. He watched with astonishment as Running Bear leaped on the horse, his speed so swift it seemed that the cold air heated as they sped by. "Damn it," Xav muttered, mounting his horse, glancing around. Running Bear was nowhere to be seen. Nothing but stringy clouds hung in the gray sky, a promise of more snow on the way. He didn't even hear the thunder of hooves.

He assumed Running Bear meant the message needed to be delivered immediately. There was no need to tell Ash he was going; she'd just worry—or worse, insist on coming with him. He checked his gun and turned toward Loco Diablo, the surest place to find Ash's renegade uncle.

ASH DECIDED THAT if there was ever a time to discover what she needed to know, it was now. The babies were napping, watched over by Burke and Fiona, in the best of hands for the time being. Xav was off riding fence or something, and her brothers were occupied with the thousand chores Rancho Diablo required.

Fiona's words had given her enough comfort to want to try on the fabled Callahan wedding gown.

She went up the stairs into the attic, turned on the lamp and looked around the big room. It appeared just the same as it had the other day, almost suspended in time. Glancing at the closet, she remembered the spark she'd thought had popped out from between the door and doorjamb, but nothing like that happened now.

Reaching for the doorknob, she slowly turned it. The

door wouldn't open, so she twisted the knob again. No one had mentioned a stubborn doorknob, and Ash was a bit disappointed. She tugged at the door, but though there was no lock, it stayed tightly closed.

There was no hope for it but to ask Fiona, which she hadn't wanted to do—she hadn't wanted a soul to know what she was up to. "Open, please," she murmured. "I really want to see what you look like, magic wedding dress."

Nothing. She'd imagined the sparks of light.

"I know Xav is the man for me, I don't need a gown to tell me that. I've always known it," she murmured, and the door swung open with a deep creak. She stared into the recesses of the closet, looked for a light to turn on.

The closet came alive in a burst of white, like flash-bang grenades she'd seen in the military, so white she covered her face with a gasp. But there was no after-burn, no pain, so she cautiously opened her eyes.

A garment bag hung in the closet, shimmering with incandescence. A gentle melody filled the attic. It called to her, beckoning her to draw the zipper down and see her destiny at long last.

The zipper slid down without resistance, the lovely garment bag melting away.

And there, before her stunned gaze, was a gown of yellow and orange, almost on fire with heat and radiance.

"Wow," Ash whispered, staring at the long train, the long sleeves, flames raging along the bodice and hem. She reached out to touch it, drawing her hand back with a gasp. The gown was truly on fire, contained in the closet—and then, it filtered to the floor in a poof of dust and smoke.

"Oh, no!" She fell to her knees, reaching out to the blackened ashes disappearing even as she tried to grab them. Her first urgent thought was that Fiona would know what to do if she could get the ashes to her fast enough. She knew how much Fiona loved this gown, she'd treasured it for years—what was she going to tell her aunt?

Ash scrabbled at the pile but it was gone, leaving not a speck behind. She wanted to cry, but that wouldn't do a bit of good—the magic wedding dress was magic no more.

Chapter Eleven

"Hello!" Xav yelled as he reached the land known as Loco Diablo. He figured Wolf or his men had spied him the moment he left Rancho Diablo and crossed the canyon, so there was no point in being subtle. "Wolf Chacon!"

A shot rang out, kicking the snowy ground up next to him. Xav grunted. If whoever fired the shot had wanted to hit him, they would have, so this was a warning. He moved his horse forward. "Wolf! Running Bear has a message for you!"

There was no one around today. Generally this land was a beehive with federal agents and local law enforcement trying to figure out how to beat back the desperadoes. Today the bone-chilling cold appeared to have kept them away. "If I didn't have a family feud to powwow, I'd be out Christmas shopping for my girl," he muttered. "Let's make this quick!" he barked at the top of his lungs. "We're burning daylight and I have better things to do!"

Something hit his back, sending him off his horse into the snow with a thud. He rolled over, a big body on top of his, and they bashed at each other with blows that were barely felt through thick sheepskin jackets.

"Damn it! Are you just a complete jackass?" Xav demanded, getting on top of his assailant's chest, sitting on him hard, his boot heels dug into his arms. "Have you ever heard don't shoot the messenger?"

"You're here to kill me," Wolf said, "you already tried. I owe you for that," he snarled.

"Well, today isn't the day you pay me back." Xav pondered whether he should go ahead and exterminate Wolf right now. It would make life so much easier for everyone.

Blast Running Bear and his peace-loving ways.

"Look. You're a mess," Xav said. "You look terrible, like you're on your last gasp. You're an outcast among your family. Do you ever think about the fact that you've thrown away your life?"

"Do I look like I need a lecture from a privileged rich boy?" Wolf demanded, sitting up when Xav finally released him. "You've had a silver spoon all your life. You know nothing about struggling, about deprivation."

Xav frowned. "Are you trying to tell me that this whole blood feud between you and your family is just about money?"

"You make it sound unimportant. But I'm like the coyote, far from the comforts, living on what I can."

"You haven't done anything to endear yourself to your family. You'd sell them out to the cartel in a heartbeat."

"True. Because all of this would be mine."

"I don't see how," Xav said, staring at Wolf. "I'm sure Rancho Diablo and all its properties are wrapped up in some kind of airtight, nonpierceable estate. You wouldn't get a thing."

"So I must steal what I can, take over what I can."

"Wouldn't it be easier to kiss and make up with your father? Not that I really care." Xav didn't. He wanted to get home to Ash and the kids. It was time to dig out the Christmas carols and mugs of hot buttered rum. "I don't care what you do."

"So what's the message? You came a long way for a man who doesn't care."

Xav shook his head. Ignoring Wolf's glare, he glanced around at the cold, snow-crusted miles of ranch, cut off by the canyons from Rancho Diablo. He'd feel a bit sorry for the old fart except he'd tried to kidnap Ash. He reached out and socked Wolf a good one in the jaw, knocking him flat to the ground.

"That's a message from me. Don't ever think about bothering my wife or my kids again." Xav rubbed his knuckles, watching Wolf hold his jaw as he lay sprawled in the snow. "The message from your old man is that you're living wrong. All kinds of mess is coming your way if you don't straighten up."

Wolf wiped blood from his mouth, looked at the bright spots of crimson in the snow. "It's too late. Nothing can be stopped, nor would I want to stop it."

Xav felt cold steel pour through him. "You're not in charge?"

"Haven't been for a while."

Xav glanced around. It was very still here, pressed in by the snowpack and the sky heavy with thick clouds. But even so, something was wrong. "Where's your gang of thugs?"

Wolf sat up, slowly got to his feet. "You writing a book?"

"That's a thigh-slapper."

"You killed Rhein," Wolf said, and Xav could see anger and hatred snapping in Wolf's eyes.

"There were a couple of girls that made up your group, maybe a few others." He looked around him, sighting the various mesas in the distance. Maybe they were all underground in the tunnels, hibernating like the weasels they were. But it was odd no one had taken a shot at him besides Wolf, and even that hadn't been a very good one. He looked more closely at Wolf. "You're on your own."

"Yeah, I am." Wolf shrugged. "What's it to you?"

"I don't understand. Did you go renegade, or did they abandon you? Has the cartel realized they'll never win?"

Wolf laughed. "They'll win."

"But not with you on their team?" A lone wolf was a dangerous wolf.

"I'm in a regrouping phase."

Xav got on his horse. "I've delivered my message. So unless you have a reply, I'm heading on."

"How do you know I won't shoot you dead and dump you in a canyon for Running Bear to find?"

"I don't worry about things like that too much." He looked into Wolf's dark, barely human eyes. "I'm not family. I stand to gain nothing from Rancho Diablo. I'm no threat to you."

"Killing you would upset my wild niece. Leave her children with no father. Put the game totally in my favor."

"Not really." Xav turned his horse to face the canyon—and home. "Sounds to me like you've got enough trouble on your hands without making more."

He rode away.

"Babe, it's all right," Xav said when Ash flew into his arms after he'd reported to Running Bear. The conversation with Wolf bothered him, but he couldn't quite figure out exactly what was wrong.

Ash hugged him like she'd never hugged him before.

"I like this," Xav said. "I'm going out for the afternoon more often."

"No, you're not. And I'm going to tell Grandfather you're not to go over there anymore." Ash scowled. "First of all, if it's too dangerous for me, it's too dangerous for you."

"Ah, my fierce lady." He hugged her to him, enjoying her warmth after the cold outside. "You missed me. It's okay. You can tell me you missed me."

"I'm in no mood to joke around. The chief shouldn't have sent you."

He kissed her. "Your grandfather knows I'm the safest one to send."

"Not to me. Not to my children." She took a deep breath. "Xav, something very weird happened while you were gone."

"Weird sounds like fun." He looked at Ash. "Are you going to tell me, or is this one of those secret Callahan things?"

"I went into the attic."

He grinned. "Couldn't resist, could you? That magic wedding dress really has you thinking about walking down the aisle."

"This is important, and no laughing matter."

"Sorry." He arranged his face into something more serious. "Tell me."

"I was going to take a peek, just a small one."

"Which is the definition of a peek instead of a look, but go ahead."

She glared. "It burned up."

"What burned up, babe?"

"The magic wedding dress caught on fire, burned to a crisp and disappeared."

That would indeed be serious. But impossible. He studied Ash's frantic face, thinking that if the gown had caught on fire, wouldn't the house have burned down? The attic was wood-floored, wood-framed, so there was more to the story. He pulled her to him. "It's okay. I think." All he knew was that he needed to comfort Ash. He was out of his depth when it came to wedding gowns, and if they were of the disappearing variety, he was even more lost. "I just know that you'll be beautiful when I get you down the aisle."

She shook her head. "I don't think I'm meant to get married."

"That's quite a leap, gorgeous. Just because a dress goes up in flames doesn't mean I'm not marrying you."

"I'm the hunted one."

"Yeah, by me." Xav kissed her. "I've hunted you for years. So you can reassure yourself about that."

"You didn't hunt me. I hunted you."

He laughed. "We just had different ways of going about it. But I have an offer for you that will put all your fears at rest."

"I'm listening."

"We drive tonight to Las Vegas and get married, like other members of your family did. You don't need a magic wedding dress, because as far as I'm concerned, you'll be magic no matter what you wear. And if whatever you happen to be wearing bursts into flame and disappears, I'll be the happiest man on the planet."

"With a nude bride."

"I don't have a problem with that."

She shook her head. "That's so typical of a man."

"What have we got to lose? Sounds like a heck of an adventure to me."

It was good to see her smile. He knew she was upset about Fiona's enchanted gown, but things happened around Rancho Diablo. One couldn't get too knotted up about it. "So, what do you say we drive up there? Pretty short drive, if you think about it. We can be back in the morning." He kissed the top of her nose. "I'm pretty sure that's all you're missing to be perfect."

"A *Mrs.* in front of my name?"

"That, and a wedding ring. I can tell by the sparkle in your eyes that you're tempted. And I have a pretty decent sapphire ring I bought you, if you remember."

"It's a beautiful ring."

"So I have you right where I want you?" Xav asked, grinning. "I can tell I do. You might as well fall graciously."

She leaned up to kiss him, which he really appreciated. He wrapped his arms around her and pressed her up against his chest, knowing that here was happiness. Here was home.

"If my dress disappears, I expect you naked, too."

"Shared commiseration," Xav said. "I can go with that. Nude is good. And I will always support you, babe, nude or not, but hopefully nude as often as possible."

"It's a deal," Ash said. "I'm falling as graciously as I know how."

"That's all I can ask for." Xav smiled, glad Ash

wasn't worrying anymore about carrying the Callahan curse. The notion was silly.

And there was no such thing as disappearing magic wedding gowns—whatever had happened in Fiona's attic no one would ever truly know.

There were also no such things as family curses. If anybody's family had reason to have a curse, it would have been the Gil Phillips clan.

He had too much of his old man in him to worry about things that went bump in the night and half-baked fairy tales.

DANTE GLARED AT XAV when he found him in the kitchen swiping some cookies. "What's going on?"

"I'm grabbing some gingerbread and cookies. About to romance my lady."

Dante eyed the small piece of luggage by the kitchen door. "What's that?"

"Ash and I are heading off for the night."

"So I hear. I hear a lot," Dante said. "I heard you went to see Wolf and laid him out."

"Hardly a tap. He didn't take it too personally." Xav loaded a few more cookies into the bag just for safe-keeping. A full bride was a happy bride—he hoped.

Dante sighed. "You can't leave."

"I have to go. Ash and I have to go." Xav glanced up. "Fiona and Burke are watching the babies." He grinned, proud of himself. "Have to strike while the bride's hot."

"We can't afford to be shorthanded tonight," Dante said. "We're calling a meeting. Join us in the library."

Xav hesitated, caught by the unusual invitation to a family meeting. "What's going on?"

"A small fire was set in one of the empty barns. It's just a warning shot, but we're playing it cautious."

Ash would never leave if something was going down at Rancho Diablo. Xav began to feel the romantic getaway disappearing like the magic wedding gown. "I understand."

"Come up and help us set a game plan."

Xav slowly nodded. "Let me tell Ash. I'll be right there." He couldn't let her continue to pack and get ready for a wedding when there wasn't going to be one tonight.

"She already knows. She's upstairs. She said to tell you to hurry up."

"Blast," Xav muttered.

"Bring those cookies with you. Put them on a tray," Dante said, grabbing one and helping Xav shovel the cookies from the bag onto a plate. "No paws in bags, Fiona says. Everything has to be served properly."

Xav didn't say anything.

"It's okay, bro. You'll get to marry my sister eventually."

"Thanks."

Dante laughed. "They say the best things in life are worth waiting for."

"Again, thanks."

Dante thought that was uproarious and went upstairs, Xav following behind with the cookies.

All the Callahans were in the library. Ash came to kiss him and take the tray from him. "Sorry. I just heard what happened, too."

"I think you're relieved not to be marrying me tonight," Xav grumbled.

"Handsome, I've waited for you long enough that I

figure one more night isn't going to make much of a difference."

"It makes a helluva difference to me," he said, not caring who heard him grouse.

"Does my heart good to hear how crazy you are about our sister," Tighe said.

"Yes," Sloan said. "Now can we get down to business, or are we going to focus on roasting Xav?"

"I can go either way," Falcon said, "but I vote we get down to business."

"The fire in the barn was started in some hay boxes," Galen said. "It happened about two hours ago. One of the hands happened to walk in there and saw it, shouted for help. They used horse-stall hoses and buckets to put it out. It's pretty gutted, but it could have been worse."

"Wolf," Jace said.

"I don't think it could have been." Xav glanced at Ash. "I was just over there having a chat with him. He'd have to have practically been on my heels to get here and start it." He considered the situation. "Wolf seems to have been cut loose from the pack. I'm pretty much guessing and going on a hunch, but I believe he's on his own."

"A lone wolf is a dangerous animal," Tighe said, echoing Xav's earlier thought.

"We don't know anything," Ash pointed out. "If a fire was set by a mercenary who's not working with Wolf, we could be in a more difficult situation than ever. We don't have the resources to fight off several attacks."

They pondered that.

"Oh, hell," Galen said. "Let's just kidnap Uncle Wolf, tie him to a rock and leave him in one of his caves to rot."

They all stared at Galen.

"You're a doctor," Ash said. "This is contrary to your calling. You're tired. We're all tired. Let's give up on this for now and plan our strategy tomorrow."

"Seconded," Sloan said. "Which means we can concentrate on the fact that Xav is trying to slink out of town with our sister."

Xav's jaw dropped. "Slink! She's the mother of my children! I think I can do a little more than slink with her."

"Think you already did," Jace said, "and we consider that sufficient. Heaven knows we've all had our little surprises, but this is our *sister.*" He shot Xav a meaningful look. "We feel you can do better by her than an Elvis wedding."

"Some of the people in this room were married in Vegas, I feel it's only fair to point out, and durn happy they were to get married anywhere at all," Xav said in his defense. "We could do it better later. But I feel it's important now to get her to an altar." He looked around at the men who would be his brothers-in-law. "You should be grateful to me, after all. In the olden days, you'd be getting me to the altar with a shotgun."

Ash said, "Excuse me?"

Xav quickly said, "Speaking strictly in a historical sense."

"The thing is, Fiona will be disappointed. This is her only niece," Falcon said. "You understand that Ash's wedding will be the only Callahan female wedding Fiona will ever get to preside over."

"Yes, I see," Xav said, "but we've already got four children. It's time for me to get your sister married."

"We understand you're eager," Dante said, slinging an arm around his shoulders in a brotherly fashion, "but we're just not ready yet. We want things done right."

"Once again, excuse me?" Ash said. "Am I really standing right here listening to all of you try to run my life?"

"Yes, you are," Tighe said, "and it's important that you listen to us. We're your brothers. We know what's best."

"No, no," Ash said. "I've been taking care of all of you for years. I don't need anybody taking care of me."

"That's the thing," Galen said. "There's no reason to get married in a quickie, half-assed wedding if you're sure this is your prince." He came over to hug his sister. "If you love Xav, and he loves you, there's no reason to rush. We have time to allow Fiona to plan a beautiful wedding for you. Get out the magic wedding dress and have your special day. You deserve it, Ash."

"I don't want to wear the magic wedding dress," Ash said, and everyone gasped, including Xav.

What Callahan bride didn't want to wear the auspicious, enchanted gown? He knew for a fact Ash had been up there at least twice to check it out. And she'd told him that wild tale of it going up in smoke, but that was utterly impossible. Just like the barn, if the dress had caught fire, the whole attic would have gone up.

Maybe she didn't want to marry him. Hell, it hadn't even been that good of a story she'd concocted.

He pushed the doubt away.

"Fiona's heart will break if you don't wear her charmed dress," Jace said. "You know how she dotes on her own legend. And she's kind of getting up there in years, had a small cardiac event when I was trying to drag Sawyer into hiding. Of course, it all worked out for the best, but you don't want to deprive the aunt of her only niece walking down the aisle in serious Callahan magic."

"Ash, you always wanted to wear it. Has he told you that you shouldn't?" Sloan demanded, staring at Xav. "This quickie wedding business is for the birds. You stay right here and do the whole thing right."

"I'm not wearing the dress," Ash said.

Xav replied, "If she doesn't want to, it's her decision."

That earned him a grateful glance from Ash. Xav felt better. It was hard standing in the face of disapproval from her family, but if she didn't want to wear the gown, it made no difference to him. He had her back.

But of course she should wear it because it would be beautiful on her, and she was the most beautiful woman in the world, so she deserved beautiful things.

He looked at Ash, saw the unhappiness in her big blue eyes and realized her ham-headed brothers were right about one thing: they were moving too fast, needed to slow down.

"It wouldn't hurt to let Fiona do some wedding planning," he said slowly. "You've been through a lot, Ash. I want you to look back on your wedding day as a special day, the day all your dreams came true."

"That's a pretty tall order, isn't it?" Dante said, and the Callahan brothers roared with laughter at his expense.

Xav sighed. "What do you not get? I am marrying your sister. It can be here, or it can be in Vegas. It can be in Timbuktu, I don't care. But I'm marrying her as soon as she'll have me."

"There you go," Sloan said cheerfully. "All roped and tied, sister, ready for you to put out of his misery."

Ash looked at him, and Xav met her gaze with a grin. He felt very confident that he was wooing Ash the way a woman should be wooed, was stocking up all kinds of points by putting her brothers in their places.

Ash walked to the door. Xav straightened, waiting for her pronouncement that they were leaving for Vegas.

"I'm going to bed," Ash said. "I leave all the conjuring of baddies and staking out of Uncle Wolf to all of you with full confidence that nothing will get done up here at all except the release of lots and lots of hot air."

Chapter Twelve

"Uh-oh," Dante said. "Boy, is she ticked with you!"

"Me?" Xav really had no good way to refute that—Ash had been aggravated. "I'm crazy about her. She'll eventually say yes to the dress idea, but she doesn't want six or more noses in her business. Anyway, I know my girl, and she's annoyed with you lot." He sighed, knowing exactly why she'd told her brothers she didn't want to wear the magic wedding dress—because she thought it was gone.

It was worth a recon mission into the attic to find out exactly what was going on. "Is this meeting over? I've got things to do, and Ash is right. Nothing's getting done here."

"You're just itching to run off and get yourself in our sister's good graces," Tighe said. "We respect that. We're married. We know how to keep our nests properly feathered."

Xav frowned. "You guys need to give your sister some space. Ash will do what she wants when she's good and ready. In the meantime, I'm out of here."

He exited the library, not sure why the Callahans were so riled about their sister getting married. He'd never seen them so protective, in such a stew over their petite, precious Ash. Xav understood, but at the same time, he figured they ought to be darn grateful she was going to marry him—a long-standing friend of the Callahan family..

"I'm the man for her," he muttered, heading up the attic stairs. "Magic dress or no. Interfering, overprotective brothers or not."

But he had the feeling she really wanted exactly what her brothers had been advising: A home wedding, surrounded by family and friends, wearing the gown that was meant for her—the only Callahan female—to wear.

Of course she did.

Up in the attic, he jerked open the closet, cursed just a bit when it felt as if the doorknob burned his hand. That was totally his imagination running wild, spooked by Ash's tale.

There was the white, poufy bag, just as Ash had described it. He unzipped it, stared at the voluminous white gown inside.

He blinked. *Holy crap. Something's terribly wrong here.*

Grabbing his cell phone from his pocket, he called Ash. She picked up, sounding as though she was out of breath.

"Hello?"

"Gorgeous, can you come up to the attic for a second?"

"No," Ash said slowly, "I most certainly can't."

"You need to see this."

"Xav," she said impatiently, "I know what you want to show me, and while I appreciate your attempt at romance, I'm not in the mood at this moment. I'm changing the babies into warmer clothes to take them out for a bit."

The gown didn't shimmer, didn't change, didn't go poof. He shook his head. "I'm going to send you a photo of something. Hang on."

He snapped a photo and texted it to her.

"What do you think about that?" he asked.

"Oh, Xav," she said. "That's so sweet of you. But not necessary."

"What's not necessary?" A wedding dress felt very necessary to this situation.

"That you found another gown to replace the one I burned up. But it doesn't really work that way. It's not like buying another fish to fool the children when their pet fish dies."

"I didn't buy this fish—er, gown!"

"Someone did," she said patiently. "That isn't the magic wedding dress."

He eyed the white lacy material. "How can you tell? Wedding dresses all look the same to me."

"I know it's not because I saw it burn," Ash said. "Believe me, it was a horrible moment."

He sighed. "So this one won't do?"

"Not really. You can't just buy a gown for a woman and expect that she'll love it. It's got to be *hers*," Ash explained.

Maybe it was time to go back to the Vegas plan. "Maybe we could do a casual wedding in blue jeans and cowboy boots? Dress the babies up to match and take a family photo?"

"I think my brothers were right," Ash said. "As much as I wanted to disagree with them. I think we're going too fast."

"I can never go fast enough with you. In fact, this thing's moving so slow, I'll probably have gray hair by the time I get around to being a proper husband. I don't just want to live with my girl and my children. It's a matter of my reputation."

"I don't think the Phillipses ever worried much about their reputations."

She had him there. "Are you sure you don't want to come see this? I'm no expert but it may not be half-bad."

"It could be a tablecloth, Xav, and you wouldn't know the difference."

Damn, she'd pinned him again. He zipped up the garment bag and headed down the stairs to find her, phone still in hand. "I think you ought to marry me before I change my mind."

She took the phone from him, switched it off and put both their phones down. Handed him Skye, who snuggled into his shoulder as if she was part of his heart. Which she pretty much was.

"I think my brothers are right about letting Fiona plan a big wedding. I'm her only niece, and she's waited a long time for this. Somehow I'm going to have to confess that the gown and I were a terrible match, and that it didn't want me anywhere near it."

"Is that what you think happened?"

She nodded. "I'm the hunted one. The gown didn't want me to ruin the magic. So it destroyed itself. That's exactly what happened."

"Argh," Xav said, kissing the top of Skye's downy head. "Can we at least set a date?"

She kissed him, and he felt a little better.

"You're not ticked at me? Because it seemed like you were when you left the library."

"I was ticked at my brothers, who were being knuckleheads. But then I realized they're pretty much right."

"I don't know," Xav said. "I think they're enjoying watching me twist in the wind."

"Believe me, if they thought for one minute that you didn't have honorable intentions, they would have rolled you into a cave and kept you there until you agreed to marry me."

"I want to marry you. I wanted to marry you before you went away."

She put Thorn into the stroller. "That makes no sense."

"Hey, I'm not exactly lightning. But I did buy out your bid last year at the Christmas ball. I didn't want anyone else to have you." He looked at Ash. "That ought to speak volumes about how I've always felt about you. I just don't think you feel quite the same about me," he said with a sudden strike of intuition. "Ashlyn Callahan, I believe you just wanted my hot, godlike body."

"I chased you for years," Ash said. "I'm crazy about you."

"So you're ready to do the big *I do*."

"We just need time."

"If I was milk, I'd have curdled by now I've had so much time. Hell, I'd have aged into cheese. These babies need a family, and nothing else matters."

Ash shook her head, put the other babies in the large stroller. "Nothing good can come of you marrying me."

"I don't believe in curses or bad karma or jujitsu," Xav said flatly. "And even if there were such things, I'm a pretty hard-baked guy. I can take care of myself."

"Juju," she murmured, "not jujitsu."

"Whatever. What I do believe in is hearing wedding bells."

"Christmas Eve," she said suddenly.

He narrowed his gaze. "You want to get married on Christmas Eve? I can do that."

"Then tell my brothers the plans, and pick a best man."

"One of my brothers, of course. Shaman or Gage."

"Fiona can be my matron of honor." She looked at him. "Christmas Eve will give her time to do plenty of planning."

He wondered about her sudden change of heart. "Less than two weeks isn't plenty."

"It is for Fiona. She's got all her notes and routes planned. She can run a wedding like nobody else."

He turned her back toward him as she started to wheel the babies out the door. "Why are you changing your mind?"

"I just don't want a quickie in Vegas."

"But you'll still be cursed by Christmas Eve, won't you? Not that I care, I kind of like you that way, obviously. In fact, maybe I don't want you uncursed. It's not affecting my desire for you, so don't worry about that, sugarplum. In fact, it's probably got me hotter than ever. Obviously your bad-girl vibe works for me quite well."

She shook her head. "Xav, never tease about such things."

"It's hard not to. I'm a facts-and-figures kind of guy. My father was a hard-core pragmatist. In fact, some people called him a hard-core asshole, I'm just saying, I don't normally let myself be bothered by—"

He stopped at the look in Ash's eyes, quickly noting he was walking on thin ice.

"I don't worry too much about things I can't see," he finished. "So, I can tell the deacon to get his rig ready for Christmas Eve? We'd better do it really early, like three in the afternoon, if we don't want to conflict with the Christmas Eve church schedule."

"It will be all right." She pushed the bundled up babies out the door, and he stared after her.

"Hey, where are you going?"

"To see my grandfather," she said. "He hasn't been to see his great-grandchildren, and I'm going to make sure he meets them."

"I'll go with you," Xav said quickly, not wanting his tiny wife out near the canyons by herself with their four babies. He settled Skye in the stroller.

"This is something I have to do on my own," Ash said and, blowing him a kiss, she rolled off.

He was probably going to have a heart attack, courtesy of his independent wife.

XAV PACED, THEN HEADED to the burned-out barn. If the lady didn't want to be accompanied, he knew Ash well enough to understand that there'd be all kinds of blowback if he shadowed her journey. He didn't like it, but he had to trust that she knew what she was doing.

He tried to comfort himself with her promise to marry him soon.

Those two weeks were going to feel like a lifetime. Xav had the worst feeling that time was not his friend; craziness had been known to hit the fan around Rancho Diablo with the speed of light.

Xav studied the barn's blackened beams, the remaining walls that were covered with soot. The sheriff had come out to take a look and insisted on an arson team taking a look, as well. Whoever had set the fire had been too clever to leave any trace of accelerants around, nor any overt sign of arson. They were left with the sheriff's pronouncement that the fire might have been started by something as simple as an electrical failure, given the barn's age.

Xav doubted it, and he didn't think the Callahan brothers thought much of that, either.

He heard something move behind him, braced himself for whatever lurked in the barn. The fire had eaten holes in the roof, leaving it unusable until it was repaired, so there was plenty of light in the building on this sunny but cold day. Xav glanced around, tensed to pull his firearm.

Nothing but a cold, stern breeze whipping through the building from end to end. Xav walked outside, looked toward the canyons to see if he could see the jeep. He figured Ash must be planning to hunt Running Bear up in the canyons. The elderly Navajo chief hadn't been around the house as much as he had been in the past, enjoying Fiona's baking. Why hadn't he yet visited the babies?

This seemed highly unusual to Xav, but the chief had a lot on his hands. Xav shrugged it off.

He tried to shrug off the noise he'd heard in the barn, too—nothing but creaking timbers weakened by the fire.

Maybe he'd just head out and pretend he had canyon duty. The truth was he had no duty at the moment, his future brothers-in-law telling him he needed to spend time with his children. He went to the main barn to saddle his horse and then walked him out into the sunshine.

"Where are you going?" Fiona demanded as she

walked past him with an armload of Christmas decorations.

"The canyons."

"Ash went that way," Fiona said, indicating the main road with a nod. "She was trundling toward town."

He frowned. "Are you sure? She said she was going to hunt up Running Bear."

"I'm sure," Fiona said. "You're not far behind her, I'd imagine."

He wheeled his horse in the direction of Diablo and called over his shoulder, "Thanks, Fiona!"

She went in the house, and he went after Ash at a cautious canter, not wanting her to yell at him for creeping after her. She'd tell him he was overbearing, that she could take care of herself, it was a bright, sunny day and Wolf wouldn't bother her in broad daylight—he could hear everything she'd say.

And those reasons made him even more nervous.

THE ONLY WAY to find out the truth was to draw Wolf into the open. Ash strolled her babies toward the main road, and when Dante pulled up at their meeting place, she put the babies in the car seats in his truck.

"What'd you tell Xav?" Dante asked.

"That I was going to find Running Bear to show him the babies. It's partially true." She looked at her brother. "Is everyone in position?"

"Yes. Your beau's going to chew all our ears off for letting you do this."

"He's not a Callahan. Drive."

Dante nodded and pulled away. Ash pushed the stroller toward the main road, her scalp prickling. If everything went as they'd planned, hopefully Wolf would follow her right into the trap they'd set for him. As Xav had said, a lone wolf was dangerous. Now that his right-hand man was dead, Wolf had every reason to want to strike.

She heard a horse canter up behind her, turned. "Xav!"

He pulled alongside her. "Hi, babe. What's up?"

She stopped, caught.

He looked in the stroller, met her gaze. "Where are the babies?"

She sighed. "Headed back to the house."

"You're running an operation?" He sounded outraged, and she couldn't blame him.

"Yes, we are. I couldn't tell you because this isn't your problem."

She could see her big, sexy cowboy didn't appreciate being left out of the plan.

"I'm going with you," he said.

"You can't. Wolf will never show himself if you're with me."

He got off the horse, put his hand on the stroller. "You're bait?"

"I'm just drawing him out in the open for my brothers," Ash said. "It's really not dangerous at all. I'm simply a decoy."

He stared at her. "Your brothers are using you as bait? I'm going to kick their collective asses."

"He's after *me,* Xav." She rolled the stroller on. "He told my brothers a long time ago that he had his eye on the biggest Callahan prize when he kidnapped Fiona, that there was a more valuable prize than even her, which would help him neutralize Running Bear. The only thing that furthers his goal is to get to me. That's what he's been after all along."

"Why?" Xav demanded. "Not that I'm happy about this, but why?"

"I told you. If he can get to me, he gets to Running Bear. And that's what he's wanted more than anything. I knew it when the magic wedding dress burned away, and when the barn caught on fire."

"What does one have to do with the other?"

"It means," Ash said patiently, "Wolf is making his move and is determined to destroy the spirit of Rancho Diablo."

"He already tried taking the Diablos. It's not necessary to endanger yourself just to trap Wolf. Nothing will work out for him."

"He gets closer all the time out of desperation. The best way to lure him is to make him think he can win. If he thinks he can kidnap me, he'll make a mistake. And then we can sweep him off the ranch once and for all."

"I'm going with you. I can't take the chance of losing you. You're not an operative anymore. You're going to be my wife."

She was an operative. She always would be. Ash looked at the father of her children, glowering at her, not understanding because there was no way he could. He hadn't grown up all his life trained for this mission.

She had no other choice. "Xav," Ash said slowly, "you need to understand that I may never be your wife. There's a possibility it's just not meant to be, no matter how much I hope it is."

He shook his head. "Listen, darling, when and where we get married is to be determined. What you wear is obviously up for grabs, but I'm not much for what you wear to the altar as much as what you don't wear when you're in my bed. We have four little babies who need us, and long after Rancho Diablo is no longer standing, that's what will be written in history." Xav stared at her, his gaze firm, sexy, determined as hell. "You're just going to have to get good with the fact that you chased me for years, and now you've got me. For good."

Chapter Thirteen

"I have to say, I kind of admire his thickheadedness," Dante said when the seven of them gathered at the stone-and-fire ring to discuss the failed mission. "Xav's pretty tough for a suit."

"He hasn't been a suit for years," Galen pointed out. "Clearly we misjudged that."

"Put in too much time at Rancho Diablo," Sloan said. "It tends to put concrete in a man's soul, gives him focus."

"And he's certainly focused on li'l sister," Tighe said, ruffling her hair, and her six brothers chuckled, well-pleased with their observation.

She wasn't pleased at all. "I can't work when he keeps such close tabs on me. I swear I don't think he even sleeps, because he's got one eye on me all the time."

Jace grinned. "And that may be his most redeeming quality."

"You guys can laugh, but he's pretty pissed at all of you. He's not happy at all with your plan to use me to draw Wolf out. He thinks he owns me now," Ash said with righteous indignation, and her brothers about broke their ribs laughing at her.

Ash sighed and stared over the canyons at Sister

Wind Ranch. It was all so close. Maybe no one felt that but her; she didn't feel defeated anymore. The land at Sister Wind Ranch was *alive,* despite what Wolf and his men had done to scar it.

It just needed a few well-placed sticks of dynamite and some other incendiary devices to take out those tunnels for good. The feds thought they'd closed them off, but they didn't understand that all they'd done was slowed the cartel's efforts. Like ants, with one path closed to them, they chose another.

Sister Wind Ranch was going to be hers, despite Wolf, despite the cartel and despite her well-meaning husband's attempts to sabotage the mission. Yesterday could have been the day they'd put Wolf behind them for good.

Dead and buried.

Oh, heckfire. I just thought of Xav as my husband. This is so not good.

He's really getting into my head with all this marriage talk.

"If you marry him, it would give him peace," Falcon said, and they all stared at their heretofore silent brother.

"Peace?" Ash demanded.

Falcon shrugged. "One has to consider every person's goals. In your particular situation, you have a man whose life mission is to make you his wife. Just like your life's mission is to save Rancho Diablo, he's not going to rest until he achieves his goal."

"So you're saying," Dante said, "that if Ash marries Xav, he'll quit hawk-eyeing her."

"Not totally," Falcon said. "But it will ease him. He's fighting for his children's heritage."

"I see," Galen said. "Brother has a point. He doesn't

make them often, but when he does, they're worth an extra thought or two."

"That's the dumbest reason I ever heard to get married," Ash said hotly. "I'm not going to marry Xav just because he's turned into my personal bodyguard."

"He can't possibly understand entirely why we live the way we do," Tighe pointed out.

"It's worth a try," Jace said. "Hell, we all just got married because we'd finally found a woman who would stick with us despite the insanity."

"Oh, my God," Ash said. "Part of me thinks my brothers are totally insane. The other part of me suddenly realizes I could be stuck with all of you for the rest of my life if I don't seal the deal with Xav."

"Exactly," Galen said. "The best part is, you love him, he loves you. You guys have four amazing children. Family should stick together."

"It's a different kind of mission," Sloan said. "But really, what else are we fighting for besides family?"

She saw everything in a brand-new, almost blinding light. "I doubt very seriously Xav will get less possessive and demanding just because he puts a ring on my finger."

"No, but you'll have your guy, and isn't that why you chased him all those years, anyway?" Dante asked.

"Not exactly." *I chased him because he was the hottest, sexiest man I'd ever laid eyes on, and I wanted him like nothing I'd ever wanted. He swept me off my feet, and I fell for him like a stone.*

"Still," Tighe said, "you have to admire someone that's so willing to come over to our dark side. He's been on Team Callahan from the start, even if we always thought he was all about our baby sister."

"Actually, I never thought she'd catch him," Galen said, and they all smirked at that one, nodding.

"You thought that? All of you?" Ash demanded, staring at each of her brothers, seeing by their sheepish faces that the sentiment had been pretty unanimous. "You're all dumb."

"So now what?" Falcon asked.

"Now," Ash said, looking back at Sister Wind Ranch with longing, "now we plan a new mission. The one I think we should have planned all along."

They followed her gaze across the canyons.

"Ash, I know what you're thinking," Galen said, and she held up a hand.

"It's my land," she said. "It might be divided up for all of us, but in my heart, I know that's where we belong and where my children belong." She took a deep breath. "It's my fight."

"I don't know," Sloan said. "As ticked as Xav is with us, if we're going to do this, we have to involve him this time, Ash."

"I vote no," Jace said. "Ash, you could go to jail."

"Or worse," Dante said, his voice deep with concern. "You could find yourself forced into hiding. Think about the babies. Do you really want Thorn, Briar, Skye and Valor to grow up without their mother?"

What was right and what was wrong? Was not saving the land from the destruction happening to it right? Was not ensuring the Diablos' freedom a mission of dire need? What about the families who might one day settle on that land, or take their children to a future hospital, or send them to schools and libraries there? Twenty thousand acres could mean much to a lot of people. Lives could be enriched, the land a mother to all.

Could she leave behind four children to understand later her decision to fight for the greater good?

"I could take them with me. I was in hiding with them in Wild."

"You'd be found. You were found by Wolf and Rhein," Galen said. "Eventually, there's no place to hide."

They fell silent, no doubt thinking the same thing she was: what had happened to their parents and their Callahan cousins' parents? Did they regret their decision to give up everything, their own lives, their own families?

It wasn't just about Rancho Diablo. Saving one ranch didn't mean anything in the overall paradigm. What mattered were people's lives, and the spirit of a community. So many people had helped them over the years the best they could, unrecognized warriors supporting the fight silently. Mavis Night, Corinne Abernathy and Nadine Waters, for starters. They ran a bookstore and tearoom in town, which wouldn't be there but for Molly and Jeremiah's sacrifice so many years ago. People came from as far away as Tempest for their treats and the camaraderie of good friends. What about Fiona's annual Christmas ball and raffle? Certainly that holiday wonderland wouldn't be held every year, and folks came from cities and states around for the fun of Christmas enchantment Diablo-style. What about the good sheriff and his men, whose families were here, schools, which educated so many people who returned their skills to the fabric of the community?

None of that would be there if the cartel had been allowed to take it over so many years ago.

Ash shook her head and silently walked away from her brothers, leaving the stone-and-fire ring—their home in their hearts and that which marked her—behind. Her tattoo burned on her shoulder, and her spirit heated with fire. She could feel it spreading inside her, taking over, preparing her for what was to come.

She needed guidance. And there was only one place to get that.

ASH WENT INTO THE CAVE and sat down beside her grandfather, saying nothing. He was in a trance, and she could feel his spirit humming. His aura was strong, shimmering.

She closed her eyes and let the wisdom wash over her.

It was cold inside the cave, and she welcomed the crisp air. A draft blew against her face, and clumps of snow stuck to the bottom of her boots. She could smell a fire burning in the cave, the scent of wood a warm backdrop to the chill outside. The ground she sat on was hard-packed dirt, over which her grandfather had laid a woven Navajo blanket, coarse and yet beautiful.

So much of Rancho Diablo was like that. And life, too.

She let herself fall into the meditative trance, releasing her thoughts to the greater understanding.

Xav tried to edge into her thoughts, but she pushed him away, then pulled him back to her. To a man, her brothers probably couldn't understand how much she loved Xav. How much she loved the children they'd made together.

It was all worth fighting for.

She saw the magic wedding dress suddenly, beckoning from a dark lair where it was alone and untouched. The dress hung, a shadow of its former splendidness, no longer sparkling and radiant.

Silver burst inside her mind, reminding her of the wealth of Rancho Diablo buried where Wolf had not yet found it, and where it was guarded by Fiona and Burke. They had been excellent guardians.

Silver in the basement, the magic wedding dress in the attic. The Diablos outside, wild and free. The images coursed through her mind in a dark endless curl through the canyons, led by a beautiful silver mare. The one that had been found trapped in the canyons by Wolf.

They were all trapped by Wolf. The magic itself, and the spirit of Rancho Diablo, was held hostage continuously.

Time, as Fiona had pointed out, would march on, their lives stolen. And yet, life was about sacrifice, duty, commitment to the greater good.

Fire exploded in her brain, flames like those which had consumed the magic wedding dress. A fire that was determined to burn everything in its path.

But then—green. Refreshment and renewal.

Ash's eyes snapped open and she gasped.

Looked at her grandfather, who hadn't moved. She'd long known she was Running Bear's heart. She possessed his spirit, as Skye possessed it, too. The gift of spirit was something that couldn't be determined or taken, no matter how much Wolf might wish it different.

Even the seemingly smallest gifts one received in this life were gifts to be appreciated and grown, their responsibility to nurture and share.

But to whom much was given, much, much more was demanded. Those were the guardian spirits of the earth, and mankind.

Ash leaned over, kissed her grandfather's weathered, brown cheek, hugged his shoulders through the worn blanket he was wrapped in and left the cave.

Chapter Fourteen

Xav found Ash feeding the babies in their room as if nothing out of the ordinary had happened. As if she hadn't tried to draw Wolf out on her own, without even giving him a heads-up of the plan. He scowled at the woman of his heart as she held Thorn.

"It would kill me if I ever lost you," he said flatly. "Kill me deader than a dinosaur."

She smiled at him, and he felt like a flashlight had just shined on the darkest places of his soul.

"You're not going to lose me," Ash said. "One thing I don't think I understood about you is what a worrywart you are."

He slumped into a chair, picked up Briar who was waiting patiently for her turn to be fed. He grabbed a bottle and began the honors. "Worrywart, my ass. I'm pretty certain most men in my situation would have died of cardiac arrest if they'd found their petite, fragile angel out trying to beard a baddie."

Ash shook her head. "There's no reason to be so fearful."

"That's what you think. My beautiful girl acting as a decoy just about makes me pop one," Xav said. "Can we agree that you always let me know the mission?

That way I won't expire from worry, and I won't ride in hell-bent-for-leather on whatever the plans are. It's a double benefit, not to mention I'll just be able to get myself out of a knot if I know the plans. I'm not good with surprises."

"I promise not to leave you out of the plans anymore."

He looked at her, making sure she didn't have any fingers crossed. "All right," he said gruffly. "I'm sorry I was ready to go Rambo this morning. But it's my job to protect you. And these babies of ours."

"We'll work together from now on."

"Really?" He wasn't certain what to think about this more amenable Ash.

"I need you. I worked hard to catch you."

"I know. Believe me, I know. There were times when I thought you wouldn't be able to, you know."

She looked at him, outraged. "That's exactly what my brothers said!"

He laughed. "I have a bone to pick with them over yesterday's failed mission, but at least they're on my side." Briar fed so sweetly, so trustingly, and he stroked her cheek, overwhelmed by a fierce desire to protect her and all his family. "So now what?"

"My brothers say we need to get married, and then you'll calm down," Ash said. "I want you to know that I'll definitely be Mrs. Xav Phillips on Christmas Eve."

"That's the best news I've heard today," Xav said, perking up. "Tell my future brothers-in-law I welcome them to my clan."

"Likewise." Ash looked at him. "And then, I need your help with a mission."

"Anything, doll, anything." Right now, he'd give her the moon he was so happy.

"I want to blow up the tunnels beneath Sister Wind Ranch," Ash said, and he started so hard that Briar flailed in his arms, looking up at him over her bottle with questioning eyes.

"Sorry, sorry," he murmured to Briar, "your mother just threw a kink into her sweet determination to marry me." He looked at Ash. "Is that going to be our honeymoon? How do we plan this? I'll make sure you pack the proper explosives and detonating devices, and you'll make sure I don't forget a book of matches?"

"This is important, Xav. It's the only way to set the land free from the evil that curses it."

She meant to flush Wolf and the cartel out. "If this is your brothers' harebrained idea, I really am going to kick their butts."

"This one's all me. That's why it's going to work."

He looked at his silver-haired darling with great concern. God, he loved her, he loved her mind, her spirit, her fire.

"Not gonna do it, buttercup." He grinned at his charming pixie. "That's no way to spend a honeymoon."

She looked at him. "You have a better idea?"

"It so happens I don't. But any idea is better than you ending up in jail, as far as I and the children are concerned."

"This is important, Xav."

"Oh, I know. Believe me, I know. I may be late to the Callahan party, but I have some sense of what this family's all about. Family first, all for one and one for all. That's why you're not going to jail on my watch."

"Who says I would?"

"Stands to reason." He shrugged, and as Briar was finished with her bottle, he diapered her and put her in her bassinet, picked up Valor to start all over again. "You can't destroy land, even if it's yours."

"It's a rebirth, not destruction."

"Just the same, anything could go wrong, and then I'd end up without a wife. I have the strangest idea you're planning this little boondoggle for before Christmas Eve. Am I right?"

"Can't happen soon enough."

He smiled at the fierceness in her voice. "There are other ways to get rid of your uncle and the cartel."

She stared at him. "Don't you think if we had a better idea we would have tried it?"

"That's why you hired me. I'm supposed to be the canyon runner, the first line of defense."

"That doesn't mean you have better ideas. Fiona usually comes up with the smartest plans. And even if they're a bit squirrelly, they're at least fun." She glowered at him. "Xav, if you had a better idea, you'd have shared it long ago. Especially since you were the one who, as you say, was the first line of defense and practically living out in the open."

"Exactly." He looked down at his son, smiling at his brave boy growing, it seemed, right before his very eyes. He loved these children. He loved Ash. "We're going to get married. You'll get your parcel, and then nobody will care what you do with it. And then, I'll help you build the best, biggest hospital, school, library or rodeo your heart can conjure up."

"How does that change things?"

"We'll squeeze Wolf and the cartel out. Think of it, Ash, all the people who would settle there. We'll make it so awesome that people stand in line to live there, raise their families. It'll be almost as popular as one of Fiona's Christmas balls."

She settled Thorn and picked up Skye. "I think you know you're speaking to my heart when you talk about building communities."

"Exactly. And I've got plenty of business knowledge and tricks I picked up from the old man. In fact, my sister and brothers aren't too shabby on the business side, either. Just think, the Callahan legacy would live on forever. Everything Jeremiah and Molly, and Carlos and Julia, fought for would stand the test of time."

He saw her eyes sparkle, wondered if she was going to cry. But she leaned over Skye to kiss him and said, "I really never needed a magic wedding dress to tell me that you are the man of my dreams."

Xav grinned, feeling pretty much as if he'd solved world peace. "So, Christmas Eve for sure, huh? You and me—it's a date?"

"It's a date," Ash said. "There's no going back now."

"That's right," Xav said, thinking what a lucky man he was. It was the two of them against the world—and nothing and no one—could beat that.

"HE'S TRYING TO CHANGE ME," Ash told Fiona when she took the babies over to help Fiona send out wedding invitations. "Xav's made me promise not to do anything he would list as foolhardy."

"Burke always said the same thing to me. Hasn't really worked," Fiona said, and Ash smiled.

"I see his point, though," Ash said.

"He's a build-a-better-mousetrap kind of guy. Chip off the old block. And you're a chip off your old block,"

Fiona said. She addressed some envelopes with delicate calligraphy. "It will all work out."

Ash nodded. "I hope so. I want him to be happy."

Xav said she made him happy. Ash pressed stamps on the envelopes Fiona addressed, glancing at her babies in the four-seated stroller. "Where are my brothers?"

"I have no idea," Fiona said, her tone serene.

That wasn't right. Fiona almost always knew exactly what was going on with her family. She looked at her aunt carefully, but Fiona went on addressing the cream-colored envelopes in a beautiful, looping hand. Ash glanced into the den at the twinkling tree, seeing the holiday-wrapped gifts that had started to stack up under it. A wealth of stockings hung from the mantel, so many it looked like an elf sock convention, except far prettier.

She sealed some envelopes, put the stamps on, set them in the to-be-mailed pile. Fiona was awfully quiet, for her. "Thank you for planning my wedding, Aunt Fiona. It's going to be lovely."

She beamed. "Of course it will! And you'll wear the magic wedding dress, and it will be perfect!"

Ash cleared her throat. "I've been putting off this conversation, actually, Aunt Fiona, hoping I'd wake up and realize I'd dreamed the whole thing. But I didn't dream it."

"It's okay, dear," Fiona said absently. "Dreams are just our brains unwinding. Don't be afraid of your dreams."

Ash shook her head. "You've been so kind to us, Aunt. We all love you so dearly. I don't know if I could have been as unselfish as you've been by leaving your—"

"Nonsense," Fiona interrupted. "You heed the call whenever it comes. There's no point in sitting around doubting one's call. It would be like arguing with a shadow." She smiled as she neatly stacked the pile of invitations. "You'll do it when the time comes."

She had to make a clean confession, and she should have done it sooner, except that she'd desperately hoped the dress would magically return. Somehow. "Fiona, your beautiful wedding dress burned up when I went to try it on."

Fiona looked at her. "Burned up?"

"Just…set itself on fire until it was nothing but a puff of smoke." It was so hard to look at Fiona's bewildered face. Ash was so upset she wanted to cry.

"Oh, dear," Fiona murmured. "It hasn't come back?"

"I don't know," Ash said. "I haven't been upstairs. Xav went up to check on it and he said there's a gown hanging up there, but you know Xav, he doesn't believe in anything supernatural or even out of the ordinary. Has no clue what the magic wedding dress looks like." She teared up a little, surprising herself. "How I ever fell for such a practical, by-the-numbers man I'll never know."

"Well, if it's gone, it's gone," Fiona said, ignoring Ash's question. "I'll go check."

"Do you want me to go with you?" Ash asked.

"Absolutely not. You finish stamping the envelopes and stay with your children. I'm sure everything is just as it should be in the attic, so don't move."

Ash shook her head as Fiona left the room. She placed the envelopes in the pile of outgoing mail, then put the babies on a soft pallet beside the Christmas tree.

Her ears were stretched out for any sound from upstairs, but there was nothing.

Fiona returned, sailing into the den and plopping herself in front of the fireplace. "You're both right," she announced. "The magic wedding dress is gone, and there is in fact a gown up there."

Ash blinked. "Who would put a wedding dress in the attic?"

"I have no idea. Strangest thing, really." Fiona scratched at her silvery-white curls, pondered the snow boots she wore almost all the time in the winter, since she said she was always in and out, and didn't have time to wriggle into a different pair of shoes every five minutes. "I don't like it, either. It's rather ugly, I thought."

"Ugly!" Ash was astonished. She frowned as Fiona fanned herself. "Are you feeling all right, Aunt?"

"I'm fine. Just a bit warm."

"Maybe move away from the fire?" She touched her aunt's hand, but it was cold, not warm at all. "Fiona?"

Fiona sighed. "Maybe some tea, sweet niece."

She jumped up to get tea, worried. "Do you want me to call Burke?" she said over her shoulder.

"No, I'm fine, dear. Truly."

Fiona's voice sounded a bit quavering.

She hurried back in with a cup of tea and a slice of pumpkin pie. Fiona was gone, and so was Skye. Ash glanced around the room and down the hall. "Fiona?"

Something was wrong, she could feel it. Her aunt always seemed a bit fey, but never rattled, never overwrought. She looked out into the chilly darkness. No bootprints led away from the house.

She was being silly. Fiona had probably gone upstairs to get something from the nursery for the babies, had taken Skye with her. "Fiona?" she called up the stairs, then realized the basement door was open. With a quick glance at her babies, she looked down the stairs. "Fiona?"

"Here!" Fiona called back.

"Fiona, do you have Skye?"

"Yes, I do!" Fiona's head popped around the corner. "I'm showing her some things."

Fiona kept her myriad Christmas ornaments and decorations downstairs, and the colored lights she had separated by holiday and season. It was also the place she stored her canned vegetables and fruits. "Showing her what things, Fiona?"

"Just things," Fiona said. "We'll be right up, niece!"

She took a deep breath. Xav walked in, and she turned to him. "Aunt Fiona is showing Skye something in the basement."

Xav shrugged. "Go join them. I'll watch the babies. I've been planning to read them *'Twas the Night Before Christmas*."

"Thank you." She hurried downstairs. "Fiona?"

She stopped, seeing Fiona looking down at a scar in the dirt floor, a long, deep rectangle that would have fit a coffin if required. But it wasn't a coffin, nor had there ever been a grave. She heard Fiona murmuring to Skye, and she went to stand beside her.

"What are you telling my baby?" she asked Fiona.

"That she's special, and an angel, and that she will always be taken care of."

"This is the silver treasure," Ash said. "This is where it's hidden."

"Yes," Fiona said.

"Why are you showing it to Skye?"

"Because it's her heritage. All the Callahan children will one day run Rancho Diablo."

"How do you know?" Ash asked. She never felt that certain of anything.

"You're strong." She kissed Skye's cheek. "Because you're strong and the future is in your hands." She looked at Skye. "These babies make me so happy! I always feel better when I hold them."

Ash knew exactly how she felt.

Fiona turned to look at her. "You can wear that dress in the attic if you wish."

"You said it was ugly!"

Fiona nodded. "It is no magic wedding dress. But you don't need magic, niece."

"I'm so sorry about your dress, though. I'd love to have worn it."

Fiona kissed Skye's little hand. "The message was that you walk your path without magic, niece. Your soul will survive this challenge, but you're going to have to face it alone. Because you alone hold the answers to Rancho Diablo." She kissed Skye again. "We'd best go join your daddy. I think I hear his heart thundering, wondering where his girls are."

Ash glanced toward the scar in the dirt floor again. "Do you ever dig that up? Make sure the silver is still there?"

Fiona laughed, walked up the steps. "It's still there."

"Wolf would be shocked if he knew it was right under his nose."

Xav was indeed hovering at the top of the staircase. He looked at Ash with a brow raised quizzically.

"Wolf has searched the house for the silver," Fiona said.

"How do you know?" Ash and Xav followed her

aunt toward the fireplace. It had been cool in the basement, but Fiona seemed over her earlier spell of chills.

"We know," Fiona said, "because he told us. And
he's always said he'd one day find it."

The silver was buried deep, but it could be found.
"Why did you go downstairs after you looked at the
gown?" Ash asked curiously as they warmed their
hands.

"Because I understood the message," Fiona said simply. "The magic wedding dress is of spirit. The silver is
of the earth. Both are part of Rancho Diablo, and both
must survive for the next generations."

"But the dress is gone," Ash said, and Xav looked
at her, confused. She wanted to kiss him desperately,
hold him to him, tell him that marrying him was going
to be the happiest moment of her life, especially since
he'd given her four beautiful children. "It's not coming back."

"Maybe it is, maybe it isn't. Take heart that the dress
in the attic now is a gift."

"It's not magic," Ash said, knowing it was true.

"No, it's not. But it can be, if you make it that way."

"The easiest way to solve this," Xav said, "is for me
to take Ash to the wedding shop in town and let her
choose her own gown."

Ash wanted to hug him for being so supportive. "I'd
like that, Xav."

He perked up. "I'm sure I'm pretty good at picking
out bridal gowns."

Ash smiled. "You're going to say the first one I put
on is beautiful, so the adventure is over quickly."

He sat on the sofa next to Fiona, took Skye from her.

"I just think anything you put on is beautiful, so I'm not picky." He looked at Fiona. "Your hands are cold."

"Cold hands, warm heart," Fiona said. She picked up her tea and sipped it. "I've been in the basement trolling for spirits."

"Why would spirits be in the basement?" asked Xav.

Ash looked at her husband-to-be and her aunt chatting like they didn't have an audience. Skye looked up at Xav, and Xav put Valor in his other arm. Fiona took Briar, so Ash picked up Thorn and sat down to listen.

"Spirits are everywhere," Fiona said patiently. "Angels, et cetera. Do you not believe in such things?"

He shrugged. "Haven't thought about it much."

"Well, you should," Fiona said archly. "Ash needs you to understand that her world is a spiritual place."

He looked at her, and Ash felt like her heart burst into song.

"Hi," Xav said. "Apparently, I've missed the fact that you're a spirit guide, beautiful."

The room went deadly silent. Ash stared at him.

And that's when it hit her. *Grandfather's spirit lives in me, and that's why I'm the hunted one.*

Chapter Fifteen

"I thought we were going to check out wedding gowns," Xav said. "I know that's what I want to do. Some guys want to watch football reruns, I just want to see my gal in a white dress."

Ash laughed, and his heart seemed to fill up at the sight of her smile. "I'm going to take a peek at the one in the attic first."

"You said Fiona told you it was ugly. Pretty sure you could wear a burlap sack and be gorgeous, but I think the kids might be a little disappointed in our wedding photos." He pulled her into his arms. "Let's skip the one upstairs, and go get you one with your name on it."

She kissed him, and he thought he'd never felt so whole. "You rock my world," he told Ash. "You've changed me for the better."

"Xav." She smiled up at him. "Only you would have stuck with me through this whole journey. Any other man would have run off screaming."

"That's right. I'm a badass." He stole another kiss. "And later on, when it's just you and me, and the babies are asleep—"

"For a whole ten minutes," Ash teased.

"I'm going to let you give me some badass reward."

"Aunt Fiona made a wicked pumpkin pie today—"

He swatted her fanny gently. "I'm looking for a different kind of sweet. Up the stairs with you. Make it fast, beautiful. I'm in the mood for a trip to the wedding shop. If you're lucky, I may even splurge for one of those dainty little garter things."

"That would be um, exciting."

"Go." He gave her a tiny push toward the stairs. "I'd be happy to go up there with you, but I sense I'm not invited."

"No need for this. It'll only take me a jif. Go talk to Fiona," she said, her voice floating down from the attic.

He went and sat in the den dutifully. "Is it really ugly?"

Fiona laughed. "We'll know in a minute."

"How did this gown get up there?"

"I assumed you put it there."

"You called a gown you thought I bought ugly?" He looked at Fiona. "Whose side are you on?"

"Ash's," Fiona said blithely. "Although I like you very well, too."

He sighed. Stared at his children, who were all now lying on their soft pallet while Fiona wrapped more presents. His ear stretched toward the attic, waiting to hear any sound from Ash. "Sure is taking a long time."

"You know how ladies are about these things."

He supposed so. His sister, Kendall, certainly took her time when looking at fashions. He didn't care what Ash wore, just so long as he got a ring on her finger, and an "I do" from her lips. "Why hasn't Running Bear been by to see these babies?"

Fiona looked at him. "What makes you think he hasn't?"

"Has he?"

"I don't know," Fiona said, and it felt to Xav like they were playing nowhere fast. Maybe by Fiona's design.

"Need any help wrapping those?" he asked, deciding to make himself useful while his children played with their toes and looked at the tree lights.

"Oh, no. Men can't wrap presents. They don't pay attention to the details. Details are important."

"I can diaper a baby in under five seconds. Pretty sure I can put a little paper around a box."

She looked up at him, her round face pert with merriment. "Only a man would think that wrapping a gift is like a diaper. It's the beauty of the wrapping that counts, it's part of the gift, Xav. It's not entirely utilitarian."

"I guess so." Just like the wedding gown Ash would eventually wear, he didn't care so much about outside coverings. "Ash! You're killing me down here!" he yelled toward the attic.

"Sorry!" she called.

Fiona giggled. "To think there was a day when we all thought you wouldn't marry our girl."

He scratched the back of his neck. "Yeah, well. Have no idea why you folks would even think that."

"I was very surprised when you called in with the winning bid that night, you know," Fiona said, her voice low, even though Ash was in the attic. "You wanted me to keep your secret, so I did, but it was the toughest one I ever kept!"

He was a little embarrassed about that. "I just didn't want anybody else winning her. I didn't want some schlub getting the wrong idea about Ash being available."

"She was very available! But if you liked Ash so

much, how come you didn't ever ask her out?" Fiona shook her head. "Seems to me you move awfully slow, Xav Phillips, for a guy who's proud of being ruled by rational thought and not emotions."

He got down on the floor and grabbed a white box, the contents of which couldn't be ascertained but which had the certain shape of a child's toy, and began wrapping it. "I never asked Ash out because I thought she was just making time with me."

Fiona blinked. "Making time?"

"I thought she came to see me when I was camping out in the canyons because she didn't want anything more than that."

"Are you insane?" Fiona demanded. "Why are men so ridiculously hard to decipher?" She wagged a finger at him. "You put yourself through this agony. You could have told her last year that you'd won her, and taken her out on a fancy date in Santa Fe. You wasted a year of wooing thanks to your pride." She made a disgusted sound and snatched the package away from him. "While you're doing a tolerable job, it's not a thing of beauty."

Ash walked into the room wearing a white dress, a sheer sleeveless column with lace at the hemline. His breath caught. "That'll do," Xav said. "That'll do just fine."

"I can't get it off," Ash said.

"Is the zipper stuck?"

"No."

He looked at Ash, got up to examine the zipper. "It's a pretty dress."

Ash looked over her shoulder. "Can you unzip it?"

He'd get anything off his bride-to-be she wanted.

"Can't be responsible for my actions if I do," he teased, but she stood very still without saying a word.

He got down to the business of undoing the dress, making certain he didn't forget himself and start kissing her neck the way he wanted.

The dress didn't seem to want to cooperate. The zipper way stuck.

"Fiona? Can you help me with this? I don't appear to have the hang of this wedding gown." Xav stepped back.

Fiona walked over, unzipped the gown. "Probably like your gift-wrapping skills. Just a teensy bit lacking." She moved the zipper down without hesitation. "There you go, niece."

"Thank goodness! I was beginning to think I was stuck in the stupid thing." Ash tore back up the stairs to take it off.

Shaking his head, Xav sat on the floor again, took another package to wrap, and this time, Fiona didn't take it away from him. "Feisty gown."

"You're very impatient," Fiona observed.

"We've already agreed on that."

"Sometimes it's good to be patient with things you don't understand."

He winked at her. "I'm learning that all the time. No worries that I'll fail that particular lesson." He chose a silvery foil with Santas on it and began cutting the paper. "How many gifts are we wrapping?"

"Tonight, twenty. I do a little wrapping every day. That way I get finished by Christmas Eve."

"Twenty!" He added up Callahans and Callahan cousins in his mind. If Fiona and Burke gave one gift each to each Callahan child, they could be wrapping gifts until kingdom come. "I never thought about what a huge job Christmas is around here."

"You'd better start thinking about it. Have you bought your own gifts?"

He looked at his children. "I meant to take Ash shopping, but I haven't gotten around to it."

"In the future, you'll spend your Christmas Eves putting toys and bicycles together late into the wee hours." Fiona sounded pleased about that. "I recommend organization."

"Yeah. Sure." He glanced over his shoulder as Ash rejoined them. "That one was a dud?"

"That gown and I did not get along." Ash flopped down on the sofa. "I swear I think it was fighting with me."

Fiona looked at her. "Let me get you a cup of cocoa." She got up and left the room.

"So, you and I are off to the wedding shop, then?" Xav finished the present he was wrapping and looked at it with pride. "Not too bad."

"Xav," Ash whispered, "Fiona's acting strange."

"How can you tell?" He looked around to see if Fiona was returning. "Isn't she always a little eccentric?"

Ash shook her head, and he wished he could hold his hot, sexy momma and let her know that he was going to take care of her. Nothing bad was going to happen ever again.

"That gown was weird." Ash said. "I hated it the moment I put it on."

He would have thought trying on a wedding gown would be a happy experience, even if it wasn't "the one." "We'll find something you like."

"That gown didn't want me to take it off."

"It's okay, Ash. You're free now."

She stared at him, her navy eyes huge.

"What?"

"I'm free now," she murmured.

He got next to her, pulled her into his lap. "See those darling babies right there?"

"Yes."

He loved her delicate giggle. "They're your freedom. Whatever you do for the rest of your life, you're going to have four little things that want to kiss you and suck up to you and make you ugly clay pottery pieces that you're going to think are the prettiest things anyone ever gave you."

Ash smiled. "I hadn't thought of that, but you're right."

"And that's freedom, babe. They make you smile, and that sets your soul free."

She put her arms around his neck, kissed him so sweetly he felt his toes warm in his boots. "Only you understand me."

"That's right. You just remember that when you get cold feet on Christmas Eve, right about the time the deacon asks you if you're going to obey me, love only me and wash my socks for the rest of your life."

She giggled again. "I don't think that's what marriage is about, exactly."

"You're right, of course. I left out the cooking and making-my-lunch-every-day parts."

"You're leaving something else important out." She whispered something sexy in his ear that brought him right out of the teasing mood and into something far more serious.

"Keep suggesting things like that, and I promise not

to forget again," he said huskily, wishing he had his sexy girl naked right this moment.

"Here's cocoa for all," Fiona trilled, holding a tray in front of her that she set on the coffee table. There were three cups of cocoa, and some cookies on a plate.

"Later," Ash whispered in his ear, and Xav felt better as she hopped out of his lap.

Later.

ASH COULDN'T PUT her finger on what was bothering her. She had so many thoughts pushing through her mind, almost scrambling her brains. Trying on the dress had really unnerved her. It felt hot and scratchy, ugly and somehow evil. When she tried to take it off, it was as though she was lost in it, with it clawing at her, trying to keep her a prisoner in its white folds.

Which was her imagination run wildly amok. Ash looked out the kitchen window at the white-covered landscape, brightened by the pale moon. Icicles hung from the barn roofs, where the stalls would be filled with horses covered in their blankets. She shivered, wrapped a wool shawl around her more tightly. The babies were down for the first round of sleep, which would last maybe four hours.

She was too keyed up to sleep.

Xav was out helping her brothers secure the barns and putting away the animals. Fiona and Burke had gone to bed.

She lit a vanilla-scented soy candle in the kitchen and perched on a barstool. Closing her eyes, she thought about her visit with Grandfather.

She'd learned so much—but there was so much more to learn.

A frown wrinkled her brow. Everything in the house was askew; it felt as if time was dancing around her, upsetting everything in what should have been a peaceful house. She couldn't get her thoughts to calm.

Fiona had seemed so giddy tonight. Otherworldly. And that business of her taking Skye downstairs to show her the silver treasure had been odd. Why had the Callahans buried the treasure down there, anyway? It was too easy to find.

Especially with all the digging his cartel mercenaries were very good at—witness the maze of tunnels.

Xav said he thought Wolf was operating on his own now. She wasn't sure why he would have been abandoned by the cartel—unless they'd decided they no longer needed him.

If they no longer needed him, then they thought they could take over Rancho Diablo without his help.

It also might mean the cartel had information on where Jeremiah and Molly, and Carlos and Julia were. Since their only reason for working with Wolf in the first place was to find the Callahans, then had they somehow achieved their goal? And let him go. She shivered, startled by the idea that perhaps the cartel had somehow found the Callahans.

Was that why Wolf had been so quiet lately? He had no connection any longer to the cartel. But if they weren't working with him, wouldn't they just kill him off?

Perhaps Xav had misread the situation. The thought calmed her a little, pushed back some of the panic threatening to take her over. Xav was only postulating that Wolf was operating on his own. It was a hunch; it might not mean a thing.

Maybe it was best to meet the enemy head-on.

Tomorrow, she would.

ASH SLEPT IN XAV'S ARMS, secure in the peace that came with being held by her man. In just a few days, she'd be his wife. The knowledge gave her a sense of comfort she'd longed for all her life.

She drifted, thinking about her parents and how much she'd missed knowing them. Her children would always know her; she was determined to turn the tide of the past.

A gasp pushed out of her as she had a vision of Wolf's face, evil and taunting. A loner now, he was more desperate than ever to achieve the goal. No longer backed up by the cartel, and no longer useful to them, the chance to take over Rancho Diablo fired his desperation.

He would do whatever it took to force them out. He believed he alone deserved the land, felt cut out by his father, whom he hated. A spirit of revenge swirled inside him, guiding him.

Her grandfather came to her in the vision, instructing her to lure Wolf to Loco Diablo. She awakened in a sweat, her heart racing.

"Babe, what's going on?"

"Nothing. Go back to sleep."

"I can't." Xav wrapped an arm around her, dragging her next to him. "My better half's had a bad dream. I can feel your heart banging like a drum. The only solution for that is for me to make love to you."

She relaxed under his kisses, his hands skillfully easing away her fear. Her breath returned, her stomach unclenched as he charmed her terror away.

"It's going to be okay, babe," Xav murmured. "I'm never going to let anything happen to you. You're safe."

She wanted to tell him so badly about the vision she'd

had. Not a dream; a true vision. It had been clear as a
bell, full of color and sound, like watching a movie.
There was so much she didn't understand, still couldn't
understand. The magic wedding dress was gone, its
magic destroyed. There was another dress in its place,
but it was all wrong. She reached deep inside her soul,
trying to find the source of her unease, yet only her
mother's and father's faces came to her from the photo
she'd seen in Fiona's room. They'd been one big happy
family—a long time ago.

But Xav held her and made love to her, and it was
as if calm water rushed over, making her forget everything for just a while. Yet the vision haunted her, despite Xav's love. The babies were the future of Rancho
Diablo, as were all the Callahan children.

She knew what she had to do.

AFTER XAV LEFT HER in the early morning, she dressed
in dark jeans, a dark shirt and a black jacket with a
sheepskin vest beneath. She went to find Fiona in her
usual location, stirring up eggs, bacon and pancakes in
the kitchen. It all smelled heavenly, but she had little
appetite.

"You're up early," Fiona said with a smile.

"I was thinking I might go out for a bit, if you and
Burke wouldn't mind keeping an eye on the children."

"We'd love to!" Fiona beamed. "Just like the old days.
We don't get many chances to have them to ourselves."

"You're sure you don't mind? I feel terribly—"

"Ashlyn Callahan, don't you say another word!"
Fiona's face was serene in spite of the reprimand. "We
live and breathe to hold those babies. We would do
it more often, but we're trying not to be overbearing

family members while you and Xav are working on bonding with those angels! And with each other, I might add," Fiona said with a wink. "He sure seemed in a good mood this morning."

Xav's happiness made her smile. "Aunt, about that gown I tried on the other day."

"Don't dwell on it, niece."

She shook her head. "It was a magic wedding dress, too. But it felt all wrong. Evil, even. Like it was trying to trap me."

Fiona nodded. "It was a dress with bad magic. You know that there are tests in life, Ash. If you'd worn it, if you'd just been content to get married just for the sake of marriage, you'd have settled for any old gown. The bad wedding dress was a test to sway you from your true path in life. Who knows how your destiny might have changed if you'd fallen for its lure?"

Ash stared at Fiona. "Who put it there?"

"The same spirits that drive your uncle Wolf, of course. We're not the only ones who fight for good. Supernatural forces are always at work, trying to help us, but thwarted just the same by their battles with evil. Angels fight with bad angels, good wars with bad—evil is always going to try to win. Magic can't stop that. What's important is that you discerned wisely. You didn't know it, but you set your course for the good and didn't allow yourself to be tempted by an easier path."

"I'll burn that dress later."

Fiona shook her head. "You can't destroy it. Only a strong woman who refuses to be set aside from her destiny destroys the gown's evil charm. It goes to haunt another poor bride, who may not make the same choices.

Life is about choices, and we are all governed by our choices."

Ash tried to smile, thinking she wouldn't want her daughters to experience that, nor her sons' brides. But by the time her children were ready to be married, maybe they'd just go to the wedding shop in town and choose something new for themselves.

In the meantime, she would raise her children to be warriors, as she and her brothers had been raised. "Thank you for everything, Fiona. I'll be back soon."

She went out in the cold, bracing herself against the wind. With any luck, Xav wouldn't discover her leaving and try to stop her. He had that tendency to be protective.

She loved that about him.

But today, he couldn't protect her, so she hadn't told him, though she felt guilty about it.

In the paddock was the silver mare Wolf had trapped when Jace and Sawyer had released the Diablos from the underground cave. "Hello, beautiful girl," Ash murmured, and the mare looked at her calmly.

"I remember you can run very fast. Something tells me you're here for me. So if you don't mind taking this adventure with me, kindred spirit, we'll see what today has in store for us."

The mare tossed her head as if in agreement, accepted the saddle and bridle with no complaint. If anything, she seemed eager to be off and running.

Ash slipped into the saddle and left the paddock, making her getaway before any of her brothers or Xav might see her. They would ask a thousand questions and try to change her mind.

She rode toward the canyons until she got to the Sister Wind Ranch, also known as Loco Diablo, aware that

Wolf had shot at Xav when he'd come out here. But only the silence of predawn greeted her.

A flash of light drew her eyes, and she followed it. To her surprise—and suspicion—a gate had been left open, perhaps by a federal agent or someone else. She asked the beautiful mare to stay close by and, drawing her gun, went down into the opening, astonished by the size of the tunnel she found.

It led to another, then another reinforced tunnel, an underground city of concrete and steel. She passed an oven of sorts, an antiquated type of bake oven used for rudimentary cooking. Ventilation pipes appeared at different intervals, denoting the potential for subterranean life.

She pulled out a flashlight to supplement the glow from crude gas sconces. Chambers split off into different directions, and an occasional wheeled cart or three-wheeler indicated transport deeper into the tunnels, destined for Rancho Diablo.

Ash burned with fury as she took in the stronghold fortified under their lands. Wolf knew all this was here, and if he had been cut loose, as Xav suspected, then he would know he had to strike before the cartel did, in order to claim what he wanted first.

But if the cartel could destroy and take over Rancho Diablo, there was no reason for them to cut Wolf in on the spoils.

"Hang on there, little lady," a deep voice said behind her, and Ash whirled with a gasp, ready to strike.

Chapter Sixteen

"Xav!" Ash hissed his name. "What if I'd killed you?"

"You wouldn't have, darling. I'm the man of your dreams." He smiled, big and sexy, and Ash repressed the desire to bean him. "So what's the plan?"

"Why are you here?"

"I told you. I'm always going to take care of you. And Fiona gave me the heads-up that I might want to follow you. Said you had a distinctly wild look in your eyes that seemed like you had something on your mind."

Well, she couldn't fault the busybody aunt for that. "I'm going to find Wolf. It's something I have to do alone."

"All right. Whatever you say."

He grinned, and she glared at his big-shouldered self. Why did she have the sudden urge to kiss him? She should be mad at him for anointing himself her bodyguard. She was a well-trained operative, and he was a hot, sexy company-owning geek who'd worked for her family for years.

"Come on," she said finally. "But if I find Wolf, you have to let what happens happen. In other words, it's my mission."

"Got it. Believe me, I understand." He took her gun

from her holster and checked it. "Good girl. You look sexy when you're prepared."

"I have four children. Disorganization doesn't fly when you have four babies." She returned her gun to her holster and proceeded down the tunnel, her footsteps soft on the dirt floor.

"What makes you think he's down here?" Xav whispered.

She thought of her vision, and that Loco Diablo was where she had to find Wolf. "Just a hunch."

She could feel him behind her, pressed tight to shield her. "This place is a bunker," he said. "Looks like it could withstand Armageddon."

"I think that's why law enforcement has left it alone."

"Or they got paid off to do so," Xav said.

She whirled to face him. "Sheriff Cartwright is a friend of our family!"

"Different county, babe. Different jurisdiction altogether. Plus the feds have been in control of this operation for months. For all you know, there's a reason they decided not to do anything about this fortress."

She'd never considered that the law might not be on their side. But Xav was right; bribes had been known to change hands.

"I can't worry about that," she said, and pushed on.

But it angered her. This was *her* land—her family's land. Bought and paid for. Intended for the good of the community one day.

They must have walked for miles without coming across anyone, yet there was evidence that indicated people had been there recently. "I don't understand. It's like it's been abandoned."

"I was thinking the same thing, angel face." Xav put

his ear against a cave wall and listened, put his hand against it to feel vibrations. "I don't hear anything. Feels inactive. Deserted."

She closed her eyes, reached to divine human movement, or spirit force. There was nothing but silence.

"It's like a tomb," she whispered.

"So is it kinky if I suggest this is one cave we haven't made love in?" Xav asked, pulling her to him.

She wanted to melt in his arms, but the memory of the terror of her vision was too real. "This place isn't for making love. It's made for war." She pulled away, regretfully letting go of him.

"Rats," Xav said. "My problem is I'm always on Go around you."

She smiled, batted away a cobweb. "Wolf's not here. My vision was wrong."

Xav kicked at something near the cave wall, sending up a plume of dust. The musty smell of the cave was almost overpowering. He shone his flashlight on something huddled in the darkness. "Look. A tarp."

"Covering what?" She swept off a few handfuls of the dirt disguise which overlaid the tarp and pulled it up.

A pile of dynamite and other explosives lay neatly, and ominously, stacked.

"Damn," Xav said. "If I didn't know better, I'd think Jace had already been here."

"No. Jace does a different kind of party favor." She shone her flashlight over the stacked pile surrounded by a metal casing. "He's more into detonating IEDs and enjoying the select grenades."

"This is quite a marker."

"Yes, it is." She folded the tarp down carefully, restored the dirt disguise.

"Why would they put in the work for these tunnels and then lay in enough explosives to send Loco Diablo to the moon?" Xav asked.

A chill spread over Ash, stealing her breath. She felt the prescience roll over her, fogging her vision, the way it had earlier—felt the heat of fire and smelled the acrid burning smoke.

The magic wedding dress had been warning her.

Xav put his arms around her, and she felt stronger for his warmth. "If you're right about my uncle being a lone wolf now, would he destroy Rancho Diablo rather than see the Callahans keep it forever?"

Xav was silent a moment. "There's no way this dynamite is federal property. They wouldn't put in this much explosive material. It's enough to take out a small city, at least a good bit of Loco Diablo."

A sudden realization came to her, foreboding in its powerful suggestion. "It's enough to destroy *Rancho* Diablo, and everything Running Bear and his two sons and their wives worked for. All the years of hiding would have been almost for nothing. Molly, Jeremiah, Carlos and Julia might have saved their lives but Wolf would win by destroying the spirit here." She took a deep breath. "It would kill my grandfather to know he'd fathered such evil."

"We'll fix this," Xav said.

She shook her head. "This isn't your battle." It shouldn't have to be his fight.

"Babe, I signed on for the war long before I knew I was going to reel you in. Trust me, I'm not about to leave the Callahans high and dry now. With or without you, I'm staying in this to help your family win."

He kissed her, comforting and sexy, a strength she was learning to rely on.

"But now that you have a good idea of what might be coming to your family's home," Xav said, kissing her tenderly, "you're going to have to leave, babe. You and the children are going far away, where I should have left you in the first place. I should never have brought you back."

"That's a fine way to talk to the woman you want to marry," Ash said.

"It's the way it's got to be. We can't endanger the babies. Now let's get out of here before we're discovered. That would really put the capper on our wedding plans. You might get kidnapped, and I might get—"

"Don't say it," Ash said quickly. "Don't even speak the words. The evil spirits listen closely."

"Okay, babe. No worries. Let's get out of here." He dragged her back the length of the tunnel, and Ash had never felt such a driving compulsion to run in her life. The very thought of losing Xav put life to her feet, forcing her through the dark passageway.

But at the same time, she knew she was coming back for those explosives.

Just not with Xav.

"I CAN'T DO ANYTHING. He follows me everywhere, my virtual shadow," Ash complained to her six brothers when she finally gathered them together in the upstairs library the night before Christmas Eve. "My overly protective shadow. He's obsessed about small details, like the fact that I haven't yet bought a wedding gown for tomorrow."

Dante looked at her. "I would call that a huge detail."

"I'm getting married in a regular dress," Ash said. "The chief is giving me away, or at least Xav asked him to. Xav's wearing jeans and a black jacket with a lariat."

They all took that in with nods.

"I'm just telling you, so that you know and understand why I've invited him here tonight."

They scowled a bit. "This isn't his first rodeo here," she said. "He's been a good warrior for us, and he's going to be part of this family. From now on, I say Xav should be part of any family conversations. Xav," she called down the landing, "come up. We're all in agreement."

"Whatever little sister says," Jace said when Xav walked in. "Welcome."

"Here's the thing," Ash said, taking a deep breath. "This is the last family meeting in this library we will ever have. I know this."

They all stared at her, astonished. Tighe passed around the whiskey decanter, and they topped off their crystal tumblers, eyeing her.

"When you're through hoping I'll disappear and that what I said isn't a foretelling of the future, you'll figure out that I am telling you exactly what is going to happen," Ash said quietly. "Our assignment is nearing its end."

"I'm not sure how you could know this, little sister," Galen said. "And yet, I know that if you're saying it, it's probably true."

They all looked at each other, not doubting her. She knew she wasn't wrong. Every moment, the power became stronger inside her.

She reached to take Xav's hand. "I might as well tell all of you this at the same time. There's a lot to go over.

You'll have to stand in for Grandfather tomorrow. He won't be giving me away." She looked at her brothers. "In fact, all of you will give me away."

They blinked, not sure what to say for a moment.

"I'll stand in for Running Bear in a heartbeat," Jace said. "But how do you know he's not coming?"

"He's not coming because he can't," Ash said with certainty, briefly closing her eyes. "He hasn't come to see my children. He's gone away."

"What's going on with you, sister?" Falcon looked at her carefully. "Are you having visions?"

"I've always known some things," Ash said, and they all nodded, "but after the babies were born, it was as if everything became sharper for me. And then I sat with Grandfather, and the visions came even more often. It's like I live between a spirit world and this world. Don't worry," she said, looking at her brothers' concerned faces, "most of the time it's a really beautiful place."

Sloan rubbed her shoulder. "Little sister, you have to do all the hard work in this family."

"It's not hard," she said quickly. "There's so much love that I always know I'm supported." And then there was Xav. He always said he supported her. "I have nothing to fear," she said quietly. "I've never been alone."

A flash of intuition hit her. She remembered saying those very same words to Fiona. And she remembered Mallory McGrath urging her to keep fighting. "Our parents are alive and well," she said suddenly. "And so are the Callahans."

They waited, and she could feel them hanging on her every word. She listened, waiting for the words and pictures to settle in her mind. Nothing more came.

"Will we see them?" Sloan asked.

"I don't know," Ash said. "What I do know is that we have plans to make." She took a deep breath. "I went to find Wolf in the tunnels at Loco Diablo. I know he's hiding there."

"Without us?" Dante demanded.

"You let her do this?" Tighe demanded, glaring at Xav.

"Xav went with me," Ash said, and they passed the whiskey around for a final topper, looking as if fortification was quite necessary.

"You do realize," Galen said, "that you have four children relying on you. And both of you were in enemy territory." He scowled at Xav. "Brother, have you lost your mind?"

"It wasn't planned, believe me." Ash sighed. "Xav believes his mission is to take care of me. None of this can be blamed on him."

"Damn right," Sloan said. "He should take care of you somewhere other than Wolf's territory."

"Why weren't we informed?" Falcon demanded. "One of us could have gone with you."

"It was safe," Ash said. "We didn't find anyone there."

"You didn't know that would be the case." Jace crossed his arms. "Sister, you're off the case."

"Off the case?"

They nodded, their gazes determined.

"You're off the case, you and your traveling Romeo," Tighe said to Xav. "You had no right to involve her in anything dangerous."

"You're fired," Dante agreed. "Fired like a chicken on a grill."

"Don't think it works quite that way, bud," Sloan said. "Not that kind of fired."

"Well, then fired, fired, fired," Dante said. "Off-with-his-head kind of stuff!"

"Oh, for heaven's sake." Ash sighed again. "You guys are so easily freaked out."

"It's okay," Xav said quickly, rubbing Ash's fingertips in his hands. "I agree with everything you're saying."

"Well, you damn well should. And, Ash, you're channeling some kind of intel we don't want you ever channeling again," Galen said. "You don't walk this journey alone, Ash. We're in this together. All-for-one-and-one-for-all kind of together."

"The family that fights together stays together," Dante chimed in.

"I walk this journey with Xav," Ash said, suddenly more sure of that than anything she'd ever felt certain of. "He's walking it with me, in spirit, in the flesh."

They grumbled about that, but Xav silently nodded.

"You can't change it," Ash said, looking into Xav's eyes. "We're two of the same spirit."

"Let's get back to you searching for Wolf in the tunnels," Jace said. "Did you find him?"

"No." Ash took a deep breath. "We found no signs of life underground to speak of. What is there is heavily fortified, but at the moment, quiet. As if the cartel is waiting for the feds and the reporters to lose interest."

"So where's Wolf?" Galen demanded.

"I don't know. But I can tell you where there's enough explosives to light up the town of Diablo."

The room went deathly silent.

"You found explosives underground?" Sloan asked, his voice low and serious.

"Enough to make Jace's heart sing," she said. "And I don't think they belong to the cartel."

"You think that cache belongs to Wolf," Dante said slowly, "and you think he plans to blow Loco Diablo."

"I think he plans to blow *Rancho* Diablo," Ash corrected. "The dirt overlay was fresh. The explosives have been recently moved there. Difficult to predict the mind of a madman, but that's my greatest fear." What else could the magic wedding dress have been foretelling, except that Rancho Diablo was in danger, might burn to the ground and never rise again?

"Call the feds. They'll get the ATF and several other agencies involved. Get that crap moved out of there," Jace said. "Consider it solved."

"Not so simple," Ash said. "More explosives can be easily bought."

"Not without raising red flags all over some government computer somewhere," Tighe pointed out.

"My suspicion is they're smuggled. That much explosive material should have flagged computers like crazy. But it didn't. And you know that the right palms can be greased with silver."

"It would buy us time if we let the feds take care of it." Sloan shook his head. "But Ash is right. Wolf will strike again. We just won't know when. At least this time, we know what's being planned." He looked at his sister. "Good work, sis. Even if we're not happy you went there, you did good work."

"I can't believe Xav allowed you to do that, though." Galen's scowl went deeper. "You should be stronger, Xav. Withstand her wild side."

Dante snickered. "Good luck with that."

"Probably he should be as strong with Ash as you are with Rose," Sloan pointed out. "Kind of bad if you're looking in your own mirror, bro."

"It doesn't matter," Ash said, "and in spite of all your well-meaning flapping and acting like roosters, you know I'm going to do what I think is best for Rancho Diablo. And since I'm the only one who has visions, I have to go with it."

"You have Grandfather's spirit," Jace said, and she nodded.

"I know. And I have the strangest feeling Skye has it, too. Sometimes she has the sweetest expression on her face, like she knows all is right with the world, and I think she's seeing beyond what any of us can see."

They all looked at her with deep concern.

"It's okay," she told her brothers. "I'm not afraid." She took a deep breath. "Xav knows, too. He has my back."

"Good thing we like him," Sloan said gruffly, eyeing Xav. "Otherwise we'd have to kick his tail up between your ears, Xav."

"I'm doing the best I can to not bring evil here," Ash said. "I need you all to understand that. Quit being my big brothers and start being—"

"Your platoon," Sloan said. "We get it. Done."

"That's right," Dante said. "Consider us your team."

"Whatever helps," Tighe said. "Ash's army reporting for duty."

"Okay." She looked at them, knowing the next step would be difficult. "You're not going to like this, but I suggest we detonate those explosives under Loco Diablo."

"Oh, good," Jace said. "I'm always in the mood for a party."

"We discussed this before—" Galen began, and Ash waved him quiet.

"They're not our explosives. Nothing can be traced to us. They can, however, take out those tunnels, and maybe, just maybe, run the cartel off. They'll blame it on Wolf, for starters," she said, "and that alone may be worth the price of admission."

"Brilliant," Falcon said. "If that's the way we get rid of our uncle, I'm all for it."

Ash looked at Galen, who was ruminating doubtfully.

"If it meant that our parents could return one day," she said softly, "what price would you pay?"

Galen looked at her, looked at all of them. "Hell, I'd do it just so our Callahan cousins could bring their children back and live here safely. Just think—they could come home."

She nodded. "Since I'm the only one here right now with children on the premises, I agree. Sawyer, too, would agree, Jace. She stays here as much as possible with your children. But we're all either operatives or bodyguards. Our Callahan cousins' wives are good people, but they're not trained. They need real lives to come home to. And that is what we agreed to when we took this assignment."

She couldn't help the persuasion in her tone. Her brothers nodded.

"For that, I'd light the match myself," Galen said. "You're sure the tunnels are deserted?"

She understood the doctor in him coming to the fore. "Totally deserted. No animals, no people. We'd check again before we detonated. I mean, I don't really want to endorse that, I'm just saying it's an option if we find ourselves with our backs to the wall."

"I'm all for it," Jace said. "That place is going to go sky-high, and those tunnels will be history."

"And when it's over," Ash said, "we roll that land with cement. We put good back where there was bad. Hospitals, libraries, schools. Anything that would make our parents proud. They were all about protecting the community, and that's the mark we'll leave here when we're gone."

"Where will we go?" Tighe asked.

"Probably where Grandfather sends us," Ash said. "I hope one day to show my children to our parents."

The library went silent.

"Me, too," Galen finally said, and all her brothers nodded.

"That's our next stop, then," Jace said. "But brother's keeping a secret about that."

They stared at Galen. Ash noted he didn't seem all that comfortable suddenly; her big brother doctor looked out of sorts and disgruntled. "What's the secret, Galen?"

"He knows where our parents are," Jace said quietly. "I remember hearing Grandfather tell Galen that he was the keeper of the secret when we were boys. The secret being our parents' whereabouts."

"Do you know, Galen?" Ash demanded, shocked.

Galen sighed. "I've always known. Grandfather told me long ago. In case anything ever happened to him, one of us needed to know."

"Why not me?" Ash demanded.

"Because you were, like, a baby," Dante butted in unhelpfully.

"He could have told me later," Ash said. "I have his spirit."

"Too many burdens dampen the spirit," Tighe said. "Don't question Grandfather's ways. He knows more than any of us ever will."

"This is true," Falcon said.

"So can we go to them?" Ash asked, excitement filling her.

"You have to ask Grandfather. Even though I knew, I was never given permission to go. However, two of us were closer to them than you realized."

Ash felt wild flutters in her heart. "That's cruel, Galen! You have to tell us!"

"I can't. It's not my story to tell. It's our parents' story, and Grandfather's. I was just the keeper of that one secret, in case anything ever happened to him." Galen sighed. "I can tell you one more thing. That website Running Bear launched is him getting technological."

"In what way?" Sloan asked.

"He used to leave photos of the babies under the rock in a cave, and a runner took them to the Callahan parents. As technology became easier to use and access, Running Bear hit on the idea of constructing a Rancho Diablo website, which detailed the history of the ranch, the tours that are conducted here in the fall, and any operations we offer, such as horse breeding. But," Galen said, "certain passwords were given out to access a part of the website that contains family photo albums. All baby photos, and photos of the children as they've grown, are in the private family photo albums, designed for our parents."

Ash was hurt. "Grandfather hasn't even been to see my children."

"So you think," Falcon said. "I know for a fact he was here one night. I saw him slink out the back. At first I thought it was a shadow, but then I realized Grandfather had paid a call to Fiona. And remember, Fiona took pictures of your babies when we had our first meeting after they were born."

"Fiona and Running Bear!" Ash was miffed. "Those two are thick as thieves. Someone should tell us something every once in a while."

"Who would benefit if they did?" Sloan asked.

Disgruntled, Ash waved her hand. "I'm just complaining. I want to see our parents. I'm tired of living driven by Wolf."

"Ashlyn!" Tighe stared at her. "Do you realize our parents have lived it much longer? Forever? We've given up nothing compared to them."

"I know, I know. Ignore me." Ash drew a deep, shaky breath. "Motherhood has hit me funny. I have all these emotions I didn't have before."

"You want to show your beautiful darlings to their grandparents," Dante said, coming to sit by his sister. "We understand. You got some real peaches, thanks to Xav."

"Thanks to Xav, nothing." Ash knew she was being horrible and couldn't seem to stop herself as she looked at Xav. "For the first time in my life, I don't feel like an operative. I feel like I'd clobber Uncle Wolf if he walked in the door right now. I'm just not able to think rationally and unemotionally anymore. I'm at the end of my tether as far as my training. I know I'm well prepared for anything, military training does that, but I'd still smack him into the next county."

They laughed at their sister.

"You're braver and tougher than all of us combined," Galen said. "You'll feel better when you blow Wolf's underground rabbit warren to pieces."

"I don't think I ever forgave him for shooting Jace," Ash said fiercely. "I never forgave him for trapping the Diablos. I never, ever will forgive him for destroying our families. And that's why I'm the hunted one. Because I don't understand forgiveness. That makes me dark in my soul."

They stared at her, inscrutable.

"I like dark," Sloan said cheerfully.

"Think of all the good stuff that's dark," Tighe agreed. "A dark room, for one. I like to sleep."

"Dark meat," Galen said. "Tasty stuff."

"Black is the essence and inclusion of all colors, for example, if one is speaking strictly of the color spectrum," Dante said, sounding like a total nerd, a show-off, which all of her brothers could be when they went rogue nerd-ball.

Ash scoffed at him. "Even if you have all your facts straight, Dante, you're all just trying to make me feel better because I'm actually a horrible, vengeful person."

"I've never told any of you this," Jace said, his tone professor-thoughtful, "but I'm actually a film noir buff. I like the old black-and-white movies, the darker the—"

"She said she gets that we're trying to make her feel better," Falcon interrupted. "Don't be a total jackass."

"I'm not! I'm merely chipping in with my two cents' worth," Jace said cheerfully. "All this talk of darkness is making me want to break out some *Bride of Fran-*

kenstein, circa 1935. You have to admit, the bride the scientist created for Frankenstein had quite a do. It's worth watching the whole movie just for her."

They all looked at him. Xav shrugged at Ash, looking as if he was trying not to laugh.

"Jace, you might want to put the bats back in your belfry. Pretty sure they're flying around up there unchecked," Galen murmured. "But I'll add Black Diablos, because they're at the top of my list of dark things I live for. Now, can we get on with the meeting? Or have we completely exhausted anything of importance we could ever possibly discuss?"

"Probably," Ash said. "Although if you think about it, we've had some doozy discussions up here."

"We're not going anywhere, yet, Ash," Dante said. "We'll probably have more family meetings up here."

"No." She looked out the window, staring into the darkness. "No. We won't. It's time."

And just as she spoke those words, the sound of the Diablos running through the icy, snowy canyons came to them, an audible specter, louder than ever, guiding them to their destiny.

Chapter Seventeen

"Listen," Xav said, watching his lady get ready for bed. "This time tomorrow you'll be my bride, Mrs. Xav Phillips. I know your mind is on other things, but I think this calls for a celebration."

She smiled. "I, do, too." She slipped her arms around his neck and kissed him. "Thank you for joining us in the meeting. You're a Callahan now."

He hopped in bed, taking her with him, kissing her deeply. "Right now, I'm going to make love to you. Later, we'll talk about whatever you're cooking up in that beautiful little head of yours."

"Just so you know, I don't really have a plan. I was directing my brothers, putting our heads together in case they come up with a good idea. Maybe they will, likely they won't. It's okay, it helps me think things through to talk it over with them."

"Where does that leave me?" Xav asked.

"In my arms," Ash said. "Letting me do things to you that I like doing."

"Why do I have the feeling you're luring me with kisses so I don't focus on what you're really doing?" He stroked her face as his lips captured hers. "You kind of keep me knocked to my knees."

"That's so sweet," she told him. "You have no idea how a woman likes to hear that after she's had four babies."

"Those babies made you even more beautiful than ever, to me," Xav whispered. "You're an awesome mother. And I can't wait to make you my wife." She felt so good underneath him he wanted the magic to last forever.

"I love you like Jace loves old movies," she said, and when he chuckled low in his throat, she said, "I've loved you for years." She ran her hands up his back. "This feels like old times in the canyons, doesn't it?"

"No." He captured a nipple in his mouth, loving hearing her gasp and then moan, went back to kissing her sweet lips. "It's better. Because after tomorrow, we'll be married. The funny thing is, the night I put in my secret bid for you at Fiona's Christmas ball, I really won a family. Can't beat that, huh?"

She moaned again as he touched the places he knew made her soft and gentle and eager in his arms.

"You could have asked me out anytime, you big chicken."

"You were hard to tie down."

"You tried very hard to put distance between us."

"You have scary brothers."

She giggled. "You're not scared of them."

"No. Losing you scares me."

"You're not going to lose me. We're together forever. Even if we never got married, we have four children that bind us."

"Don't say that," Xav said. "Don't even speak the idea that we might not get married. I've learned around

Rancho Diablo that word is deed. It's something in the water or something, but a man's word turns into action. Like that crazy magic wedding dress. One day it's a fairy-tale gown, the next day it's dust. Sometimes I thought there was a conspiracy against us."

"No conspiracy," Ash said. "Now make love to me and quit worrying. You're borrowing trouble."

He hoped he was. He probably was. Xav tried to forget all about the strange sensation he had that something just wasn't right, and lost himself in loving Ash.

ASH AWAKENED IN THE NIGHT, the same dream haunting her. She peered at Xav, who slept soundly, his handsome profile just visible in the moonlight streaming through the window. One leg draped over the side of the bed, as if he were ready to spring into action if the babies called.

She went to the foot of the bed to look at them in their baskets. They slept soundly, everything right in their world. Just the sight of them reassured her. She adjusted their blankets, amazed that somehow today was her wedding day, and the day before Christmas.

She was a mother, and she would be a wife. Here in this room was her family, who meant more to her than anything. All in the space of a year, she'd been blessed with more than she'd ever dreamed of. So far from the days when she'd been a girl going into the military, struggling to make sense of herself and who she was to be in the world. Now she had all the pieces of herself she could ever need. With Xav and her babies, she was whole.

It was a miracle, one she deeply appreciated.

Glancing at the clock, she saw that it was only four in the morning, not quite time for Xav to be up for chores. She decided to go downstairs and put the coffee on, get a jump on Fiona's breakfast preparations. She pulled on jeans, put on her rubber-soled black boots, grabbed a black T-shirt and sheepskin jacket, smiling at the thought that these were hardly the clothes of a bride.

But she had a pretty blue dress for later, and while it wasn't the magic wedding dress, she would still become Mrs. Xav Phillips.

It was a most magical and exhilarating thought.

She turned on the coffeepot, set out some small dishes for muffins and breakfast cake. Put on the teakettle for herself. Grandfather always preferred tea, she thought with a smile. He wasn't one for coffee. Running Bear loved sitting in this kitchen with Fiona, chatting and drinking tea. Plotting.

Those two had certainly worked hard for everything that was Rancho Diablo. Ash looked around the kitchen, hardly able to wait until sunlight came pouring in the many windows to herald Christmas Eve.

Her babies' first Christmas.

Joy sparkled inside her—disappearing when a shadow crossed one of the windows. Something about the shadow caught her attention, alarming her. A ranch hand wouldn't walk so stealthily, and Running Bear would just walk in the back door that led to the kitchen. None of her brothers would be at the house yet. Fiona and Burke wouldn't come down until closer to five o'clock.

Her blood running a bit colder than it had a moment before, she opened the door, peering out.

There was nothing there, no prints in the fresh, bright snow visible in the porch light.

Ash breathed a sigh of relief, closed the door. Poured herself tea, grabbed a zucchini muffin. Tried to shake off the chilly sensation that had come over her.

She hadn't been wrong about Wolf. She knew he was planning to blow something, but whether Rancho Diablo or Loco Diablo she couldn't be certain. That had not yet been revealed to her. But with one of the barns being set on fire before, it made sense that Rancho Diablo was under siege.

Under siege. Of course it was. They just hadn't realized the war had begun and was right at their doorstep.

She ran to head up the stairs to get Xav, tell him that they needed to get the babies to safety, when something grabbed her out of nowhere, fingers biting hard into her shoulders as something cold landed across her mouth.

Velvety blackness descended upon her.

XAV SAT UP IN BED, his heart hammering. He'd heard something, felt something eerie, a warning thrusting him into instant wakefulness. He jumped out of bed, checked the babies. Ash was probably showering—but no. She wasn't there, and her boots were gone.

He texted her, pulling on his clothes while he waited for a response. His gaze lit on her phone suddenly, on the nightstand, turned off. He wanted to hurry downstairs to check the kitchen, but leaving the babies alone wasn't an option. The babies slept soundly, completely secure in their cozy worlds. Only Skye stirred, opening her eyes once to look at nothing in particular, then went back to sleep.

He texted Burke and Fiona.

Can you come sit with the babies for a minute?

It wasn't sixty seconds before Fiona flew down the long hall, Burke at her back.

"Mercy!" Fiona exclaimed. She wore a pink robe and tiny curlers in her silvery-white hair. "Is everything all right?"

"Everything's fine. I need to find Ash. I'll be right back."

"Isn't she in the kitchen?" Fiona asked. "I should be there now, making breakfast."

"For now, stay up here. Let me make certain I just woke up with a case of the heebie-jeebies and nothing more serious is going on." Xav checked his gun, slid it into his holster. "Once I find my bride, I'll know I had an epic panic attack."

"Panic is good," Fiona said. "Sometimes the subconscious knows more than we think. Go. Burke and I can handle our adorable angels." She went over to peer into the bassinets, and Xav hurried downstairs.

She wasn't in the kitchen, as Xav had somehow known she wouldn't be. But maybe she'd gone to the barns.

Maybe all the Callahan hocus-pocus was getting to him, but he'd swear he was picking up some kind of fear communication from his wife. His scalp tingled and it felt as if ants were crawling all over his skin.

His gaze lit on a muffin, with one bite taken, and a mug of tea barely sipped and still hot.

She wouldn't have left the kitchen this way.

His heart shifted into extreme fear, and he pushed it away. Texted her brothers. Can't find Ash.

Instantly, six texts hit his phone.

On it, from Jace.

Locked and loaded, from Dante.

From Tighe's phone: Time to kick some ass.

Galen's text read simply, Hang tight.

Stay calm, from Sloan.

On my way, Falcon's text said.

Xav felt a little better with the instant backup. He checked the kitchen door, looking out in the snow for footprints, signs of a struggle. Went to the front door, saw sweeping motions in the fresh snow. Ash had put up a good fight, her boots scrabbling as she'd kicked at her captor. Fresh anger poured over him, whipping him into a red-hot desire to put Wolf out of his misery— and theirs.

"Fiona!" Xav yelled up the stairs.

Fiona's rollered head and pink robe appeared at the top of the stairwell. "Find her?"

"Get the babies. You and Burke go in your room and lock the doors."

Her eyes went wide. She scurried down the stairs. "I have to grab bottles for the babies!" She threw several into her robe pockets and disappeared into the secret elevator, a whirl of motion.

Xav pulled on his jacket and hat, grabbed a gun from the locked gun cabinet in the kitchen, not surprised when the kitchen doors burst open a second later and Callahans spilled in. They stamped their feet on the floors, glancing around, scoping everything for information, in instant military mode.

"What's happening?" Sloan demanded.

"Whoever grabbed her took her through the front."

"Then we'll have him in five. Good work, brother," Jace said, and hauled ass out of the kitchen with his fierce brothers.

Yet something held Xav back. He glanced at the door they'd come through, went to it, trying to figure out what was niggling at him. He knew Ash had been taken out the front.

He stepped out the back anyway, not sure exactly what was bothering him. Saw someone in the shadows throw something fiery through the kitchen window.

He ran back inside. A bottle lay on the kitchen floor, smoking from the flames inside it. It should have burst, should have lit the kitchen into an instant inferno. He knew what it was, knew he had a limited time to get it out of the house. Maybe he wouldn't even make it— but he had to try. His children were upstairs, as well as Fiona and Burke.

In a split second, he'd thrown a heavy cast-iron pot over the Molotov cocktail, smothering it as it belched flames underneath it. He grabbed Fiona's fire extinguisher, putting out the flames. Dialed the sheriff to let him know they needed backup and coverage on the house—then called Galen.

"They took Ash out the front as a decoy, knowing we'd give chase, then threw a Molotov cocktail through the kitchen window."

"Holy hellfire," Galen said. "Is everything all right?"

"It is now." It had been close—too damn close. "I'm going to stay here until the sheriff arrives. You get Ash."

"Dante and Tighe are riding back with Ash right now. They found her walking back, pissed as hell and sporting a gash on her cheek. She doesn't take well to being dragged off against her will."

"Who did it?" If it had been Wolf, he'd be lucky to still be alive—Xav was going to take him out with his bare hands.

"Dante said it was two henchmen. By the time Ash nearly bit off her captor's finger and kicked his knee-cap almost to China, he was ready to get rid of her. His buddy lit off when she said if he so much as moved she was going to do something to his balls that would leave him singing like a girl for the rest of his life. Wolf must not pay enough to make the job worth it, because I don't think their hearts were in it. Then again, Ash is scary when she's ticked."

"That's my girl." Xav grinned proudly, relieved, but still seething and ready to kick some Wolf ass. He had the sexiest spitfire in New Mexico. Hell, in the whole country. "Thanks, Galen."

"Thanks for keeping Rancho Diablo from burning to a cinder."

He heard a gasp and Ash's sweet voice came on the phone. "Xav! Are you all right? What happened?"

He got a blinding rush of relief at the sound of her voice. "It's all right. Someone threw a parting gift through the kitchen window. Fiona got a little something in one of her pots she won't be too happy about, but fortunately, cast iron does a good job of containing an incendiary device."

"I'm going to kill him," Ash said.

"You can't," Xav said. "We don't know that it was Wolf. Could have been the cartel. Dante and Tighe said you were taken by a couple of henchmen, and I didn't know the asshole who tossed the cocktail. I didn't get a good look at him."

"It's Wolf's fault for bringing them here. He's the reason the cartel got so dug in. He's the reason everything has been screwed up for so long, for all of us. And will be for our children, all of our children. Galen, don't try to stop me."

"Galen? What just happened?" Xav said, as Galen came back on the line.

"Ash took off. She grabbed Jace's horse and she's gone."

"I know where she's going," Xav said. "She's going to the tunnels, and I wouldn't be surprised if she's thinking to set off that dynamite. Stay with her. I'll catch up."

He knew exactly what his bride-to-be would do.

ASH RODE HARD through the canyons to Sister Wind Ranch, snow flying from the horse's hooves. She knew her brothers were hot on her trail and that was fine. They should be with her. This was the moment for which they had come to Rancho Diablo. Just knowing that someone had intended to burn it down—with her family in it—pushed her past the point of reason.

There was no forgiveness for Wolf now.

She leaped off Jace's horse at the mouth of the tunnel she and Xav had gone in. Hurrying through the maze of cold dark passageways, she didn't even try to be silent and unseen.

As she'd expected, Wolf was in the tunnel.

"Hello, niece."

"Get out of my way, Uncle Wolf."

He smiled. "You're here because of my housewarming gift."

Housewarming. He was laughing at her, at her family. "My children were in that house, you miserable scum. I don't know why Grandfather won't let us kill you. You have no soul." She wanted to murder him in the worst way, felt her grandfather's spirit settle over her, taking the edge off her boiling rage.

He shrugged. "Running Bear protects me because he is weak. My father is always hoping the prodigal son will come back to the family fold."

"He certainly gave you enough chances to do so. Why didn't you?"

"Because," Wolf said, his voice deep with determination, "my brothers are in hiding. They can never claim anything. Everything will come to me. All that's standing in my way is Running Bear—and you. Running Bear is old. He can't last forever. And you," Wolf said calmly, "you're just a girl. And in spite of your brave words, you won't go against Running Bear's teachings. You won't harm me."

He smiled, confident and chilling.

"You could have *killed* my children," Ash said. She thought about the gown burning away, a sure warning; she thought about the Diablos being trapped to be sold for God only knew what purposes, and she thought about this man almost killing Jace. She thought about her parents' suffering and the Callahan cousins', and she thought about the family life they'd never had—and she pulled out a gun and pointed it at Wolf's boots. "Run."

"You won't shoot. All this dynamite will go up in a fireball."

"Let's not test her," Xav said behind her. "She's not in the best of moods. In fact, her mood is distinctly not favoring you at the moment. And neither is mine. So if she doesn't get you, I probably will."

Her brothers suddenly appeared around her.

"She doesn't have to shoot you," Dante said. "I'll do it." He drew a gun, as did his brothers.

Wolf's eye widened. "You'd all die with me."

"Then we'll all go to Hell together. Run *fast,*" Xav said again, and Ash fired one single shot between Wolf's boots, and Wolf took off running.

"Follow him, Jace," she said, her voice cold. "Everybody out of the tunnel. Get far, far away."

"Let me handle this part, sister," Jace said. "As you know, this is something of my specialty." He looked at the neatly stacked contraband. "In fact, the Great Spirit probably let me live just so I could enjoy this moment."

She nodded. "Give us to the count of sixty. And you get the hell out, too. Don't piss me off by dying or getting some fingers blown off."

They hurried from the tunnel, Xav pulling her along.

"The wedding's going to seem a bit anticlimactic for you," Xav said as they ran.

"Anticlimactic sounds heavenly." She looked behind them, then mounted Jace's horse. "Everybody ride like hell for the canyons."

She glanced around for Wolf. Sure enough, his bony body was running as fast as he could in the chewed-up snow, hightailing it for safety.

She wanted to ride him down, but didn't. Focused on the rules Grandfather had given them, reminding herself that his spirit resided inside her.

On a high mesa visible now in the dawning sun, she saw Grandfather, realizing she'd expected him to be there. Knew he would be there. He stared down at them, watching the battle unfold, waiting.

She turned, waiting for Jace to make it out.

"He's going to be fine." Xav pulled up beside her. "Fireworks are never going to seem quite the same after Jace sets his off."

"Come on, Jace," she murmured. "Get out of there."

She saw Jace riding like the wind, galloping hard toward the canyons on the back of the silver mare, swifter than any horse she'd ever seen run.

"Go," she said under her breath. "Come on!" she screamed at the top of her lungs, knowing it couldn't be much longer before Armageddon let loose.

She glanced toward Wolf, seeing that he'd stopped, too, was watching behind him—then gasped when he raised a gun to his eye to fire on Jace.

"Xav! He's got a gun!"

They were all carrying pistols. Wolf had brought a long-range rifle with him or he'd had it hidden among the rocks, and he sighted Jace, too far from the Chacon Callahans to do anything about it. She knew Jace couldn't possibly see that he was in the crosshairs.

Xav took off, his horse streaking across Wolf's line of vision. Ash stared, horrified, as Xav drew Wolf's attention, the rifle following Xav now, Wolf sighting him. Her heart shriveled, her breath stopped—and suddenly, a fierce dust storm rose from nowhere, a sweeping funnel skirting and driving along the ground toward them.

She glanced at Running Bear, saw him watching, his arms raised high. The funnel danced on the ground, gathering speed and power, swirling with dark wind and dust and rotational kinetic energy. A sudden horrific boom rose from underground, shaking everything around her and her brothers, startling the horses. Dust and snowy dirt clumps flew as the tunnels collapsed, and Wolf lowered his rifle for a moment, staring at the hellish vengeance Jace had unleashed.

Ash momentarily worried that even the canyons might fall in, their walls, strong for thousands of years, not capable of withstanding the force.

But they held, as did the mesa where Running Bear rose on the back of his horse, his arms stretched high. An eerie cry, a wordless keening song, filtered to them on the winds from the gathering tornado wall.

"Damn, Jace," Galen said. "That was a beauty," he said as his brother gained their side.

"Have to say she was a sweetie," Jace said proudly. "I can still set a charge like a pro. He had everything I needed to take out a good many of the tunnels. All I needed was fast feet and a prayer."

"You're a pro," Dante said, high-fiving him.

"Nobody better," Jace bragged proudly.

Ash screamed, realizing Wolf had raised his rifle again, his momentary disconcertment gone in his eagerness to take out a Callahan. Xav rode toward Wolf, his purpose clear. He was going to force Wolf off the edge, send him into the canyon below, and Ash's heart barely beat as she watched Wolf squeeze off a shot at the man she loved. Unable to take it another second, she rode at Wolf hard, hearing her brothers yell for her to stop.

She could get to Wolf first, drive him into the canyon before he hurt Xav. It was time, the moment was on her, and the knowledge urged her on.

The funnel burst in a fury of hot, dry desolation, blowing sand and grit and the heat of unholy fire into her, driving her back. She gasped against the power of it, saw Xav riding strong despite the funnel's fury—a fury which suddenly engulfed Wolf, sucking him into its vortex and sending him into the canyon below.

The funnel danced along the bottom of the dry arroyo, swirling and magnificent. Ash rode to Xav, jumped off her horse to pull herself up on his horse and into his arms. He held her, wrapping her against his big, strong chest.

"It's over," Xav said. "Babe, it's over. He's not coming back."

She looked back at Running Bear atop the mesa. The chief sat there, proud and strong, unmoving as he watched the funnel leave the canyon, a spirit wind guiding itself to places unknown.

Then he turned and rode away.

Chapter Eighteen

Christmas Eve came frosted with light snow that dusted the tops of the corrals amidst the white holiday lights, and snowflakes that glittered on windowpanes, giving Rancho Diablo a fairy-tale glow. Ash smiled as she looked at herself in the mirror, her knee-length blue dress paired with tan suede boots, and a bridal bouquet of white roses tied with a silver ribbon.

"Your hair looks lovely, if I do say so myself," Fiona said, twining a silver ribbon through the fall of Ash's platinum hair. "You're a beautiful bride. I wish you could wear the magic wedding dress, but all the same, this is a magical day for you."

Ash turned to hug Fiona. "Thank you for agreeing to be my matron of honor, dearest Aunt."

"Have I ever received a greater honor!" Fiona beamed, and they looked at the babies wrapped in matching white blankets with tiny silver ribbons glimmering throughout. The babies wore darling onesies of soft velour, an ivory color Fiona said was fit for a wedding.

"Thank you for everything you've done for me," Ash murmured, looking at her children, thinking about how they'd benefited from Fiona's plentiful caring. "You and Burke have been the parents I never really had."

Fiona looked pleased. She patted Ash's hair one last time and turned to pick up a baby.

"Where will you go now, Fiona? Will you stay here?"

"I don't know. The Callahans will come home, and that'll give this heart something to be overjoyed about. And you will all build on Sister Wind Ranch, so you'll be settled nearby."

"We'll build you and Burke a house," Ash said suddenly. "I couldn't bear it if you went too far away. And my children should know their wonderful great-aunt and great-uncle."

"I'm sure we'd be pleased to take you up on that offer." Fiona nodded. "I'm glad you're marrying Xav. He's taken on the Callahan way of life without any doubts."

"I'm so in love with him, Fiona." She remembered the panic in her heart as Xav had raced to save Jace, and knew she'd found the only man whom she could ever love.

"He's in love with you, too, my girl. Good things come to the good," she said happily.

"I'm not good," Ash said, her voice soft.

Fiona touched her cheek. "Dear girl, you were always good. We fight the battles we must. Anyone who puts themselves on the line for the greater good is deserving of peace and calm in their soul."

"I didn't think I would feel peace and calm," Ash said, "but not only do I feel peaceful and happy, I feel secure. Blessed. Like everything happened for a reason, even if I couldn't understand that at the time."

Fiona smiled to herself. "Let's go find your handsome groom."

Ash looked one more time at the blue dress. It was pretty, she'd loved it when she chose it, but it did seem strange to be the only Callahan bride never to wear Fiona's treasured gown.

"I wish I could have worn your magic wedding dress, Fiona," Ash said, reaching out to hug her darling aunt who'd done so much for her.

And no sooner did she speak the words but a melody began playing, soft and lilting, surrounding her with its joy. Tiny trembles of magic bounced and glittered along her hem and the sleeves of the blue dress, and as she watched, the dress transformed itself into a beautiful white wedding dress, a sweeping train and a lovely sheer veil shimmering and evanescent. She gasped, looking at her feet, adorned in sexy pumps that sparkled with enchantment.

"Fiona, look!"

"I see," Fiona said, laughing with delight.

And if Ash hadn't known better, she would have thought she saw her aunt tucking away a wand, hiding it from view as she smiled at her, as if dresses so beautiful appeared out of thin air every day.

Of course there was no wand. That would be a fairy tale—and Ash was already living one of those.

"Thank you, Fiona," she whispered, hugging her aunt to her. "I love you so very much. I'm the happiest woman in the world!"

And suddenly, in the mirror, Ash saw Xav smiling at her. He reached out to take her hand, and when she expected to feel his touch, she felt only his warmth and love before the vision in the mirror disappeared.

It was all magic, of course. The magic of love and the belief that anything could happen—any miracle at all.

Whatever your heart could conceive of, that was the dream you had to fight for. And Ash knew she'd been blessed with Xav, and her children, and a family who loved her.

Forever.

"Wow," XAV SAID when Ash came down the aisle, escorted by her six brothers, which might have freaked out a lesser groom, but now just seemed normal. Callahan-normal.

Besides which, his bride was so gorgeous he couldn't even look at her tux-wearing escorts. He knew instantly she was wearing the magic wedding dress—she glowed with happiness and joy. A few people he didn't know held his babies in the white chairs Fiona had put in the house for the occasion, but if Fiona trusted these folks, then they had to be all right. He recognized Mallory McGrath from Wild, Texas. Ash would be delighted that Mallory was there. Their Callahan cousins and their wives and children could have filled up a small church on their own, and Xav was amazed by all the people from the town of Diablo who had come out on this Christmas Eve to see them married.

Ash came to stand beside him, and he couldn't help himself. He kissed her soft pink lips right in front of the deacon and all the guests. "You are the most beautiful bride in the world."

She smiled. "Not the world."

"My world, babe. Yes, you are. And all mine, at last." Xav drew in a heavy breath. "I can't believe it's finally going to happen. You're going to become my wife." He looked at the deacon. "Am I the most fortunate guy in the world or what?"

The deacon smiled. "I'll begin the ceremony now, if you'd like, Mr. Phillips."

"The sooner the better, Deacon. Thank you." He grinned at Ash. "And you thought the magic wedding dress was gone forever."

She smiled up at him, adorable and sexy and his true soul mate.

He kissed her hand. Whispered for her ears only, "Hottest bride in New Mexico."

Ash blushed furiously. He grinned again, knowing her heart was his. Finally, after the years he'd spent tearing through her walls, she was going to belong to him. And he to her.

Her brothers eyed him with knowing smiles, understanding exactly the depth of his emotions.

"I'm going to have some help today in this blessing," the deacon said. "Chief Running Bear has graciously agreed to officiate with me in a combined Navajo ceremony."

"Grandfather," Ash said, her eyes lighting with happiness, "thank you for this wonderful gift."

Running Bear's dark eyes shone on his only granddaughter and Xav knew the chief was thinking that his granddaughter had his spirit, his heart. It was perfect that he bless their wedding, and when the chief fed them both some blue cornmeal, Xav felt Ash's joy. The deacon asked who gave this bride to be married, and her six brothers said, "We do!" in voices so loud and strong that the guests giggled.

Ash laughed, too, and Xav kissed her hand as her brothers took their seats.

A man stood up in the audience, his wife beside him. He held Valor, and his wife held Skye. "Her mother and I also join in giving our daughter in marriage."

Everyone gasped. Ash whirled to face the people who'd spoken. She would have known Julia anywhere; she looked like her in so many ways. And her father was tall and strong, if a little gray around the temples.

She felt their life force as they smiled at her. Had felt it before—months ago in Colorado when she'd gone to see Sawyer and Jace. In the cabin in the mountains, where she'd had the strongest sense that the house they stayed in was a happy home, a sanctuary.

She had a family. Her brothers and she had a family.

"Oh, my God," Ash murmured, trying not to weep tears of thankfulness. She beamed at her parents, and they smiled at her as they took their seats again.

"Here, babe," Xav said, holding her close to him. Her hands shaking, her bouquet quivering, she proclaimed her love for her husband, and as Xav put the beautiful diamond-and-sapphire ring on her finger, Ash knew that dreams really did come true, dreams that were spun from hope and love.

And a little bit of magic.

AFTER THEY WERE pronounced husband and wife, Xav led Ash down the aisle to the applause of their guests—but he wasn't surprised at all when Ash flew into her parents' arms. He stood back, grinning, completely understanding the miracle Ash had received. He watched his beautiful bride and her brothers surround their parents, the family hugging and kissing each other, and he, like the other guests, knew they were witnessing a very special moment.

And if he hadn't thought another miracle could come their way that night, a woman came over to them, hugging first Julia and then Carlos.

"Mallory McGrath!" Ash exclaimed.

Mallory smiled. "Actually, my name is Molly Callahan, and this is my husband, Jeremiah," she said, holding Briar as Jeremiah held Thorn, and people rushed to welcome the Callahans and join in the reunion and the celebration as the Callahan cousins hugged their parents, too.

It was a miracle, a true miracle, and the seven-chimneyed house at Rancho Diablo practically filled with joy and laughter and tears and happiness. There was nothing more needed, no greater blessing could be had.

Ash held his hand, turning to look at him. "You gave me this moment."

"Beautiful, this moment is all yours. Yours and your families'. You worked hard for it. I get to be the lucky man marrying you."

"I'm so very blessed by you, and our children," she said, her voice full of love. She looked around the room as everyone celebrated each other, long-lost friends and families sharing a special Christmas they thought would never come.

It had, at last.

She smiled happily at Running Bear, and he winked. In the distance she heard thundering hooves, running free and wild, and shimmers filled the room, even touching the Christmas tree with miraculous, beautiful light.

She and Xav shared a long, sweet kiss, knowing their

love was truly blessed—by family, by friends, by everything that was strong and true.

Maybe in some other parts of the world, sand or dust mysteriously blown by ephemeral winds beat against hard unforgiving walls, helplessly yearning to get inside, but here, this night, the spirits danced with pure joy.

The Callahans kept the legend, always.

* * * * *

COMING NEXT MONTH FROM

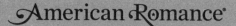

HARLEQUIN®

American Romance®

Available May 6, 2014

#1497 ONE NIGHT IN TEXAS
by Linda Warren

Telling the truth about her child's paternity could destroy Angie Wiznowski's relationship with her daughter *and* her daughter's father. But it was a secret Hardison Hollister was never meant to know....

#1498 THE COWBOY'S DESTINY
The Cash Brothers
by Marin Thomas

Destiny Saunders is pregnant and determined to raise her baby on her own. When cowboy Buck Cash arrives in town, Destiny knows nothing can happen between them. Even if she really wants it to!

#1499 A BABY FOR THE DOCTOR
Safe Harbor Medical
by Jacqueline Diamond

Handsome surgeon Jack Ryder had a reputation as a ladies' man until he met the one woman who refused to be impressed: nurse Anya Meeks. She's carrying his baby—and she's determined to give it up for adoption.

#1500 THE BULL RIDER'S FAMILY
Glade County Cowboys
by Leigh Duncan

Chef Emma Shane took a job on the Circle P Ranch to provide a quiet home for her young daughter. But former bull rider Colt Judd is making her life there anything but peaceful!

REQUEST YOUR FREE BOOKS!
2 FREE NOVELS PLUS 2 FREE GIFTS!

HARLEQUIN®

American ★ Romance®

LOVE, HOME & HAPPINESS

YES! Please send me 2 FREE Harlequin® American Romance® novels and my 2 FREE gifts (gifts are worth about $10). After receiving them, if I don't wish to receive any more books, I can return the shipping statement marked "cancel." If I don't cancel, I will receive 4 brand-new novels every month and be billed just $4.74 per book in the U.S. or $5.24 per book in Canada. That's a savings of at least 14% off the cover price! It's quite a bargain! Shipping and handling is just 50¢ per book in the U.S. and 75¢ per book in Canada.* I understand that accepting the 2 free books and gifts places me under no obligation to buy anything. I can always return a shipment and cancel at any time. Even if I never buy another book, the two free books and gifts are mine to keep forever.

154/354 HDN F4YN

Name _____ (PLEASE PRINT)

Address _____ Apt. #

City _____ State/Prov. _____ Zip/Postal Code

Signature (if under 18, a parent or guardian must sign)

Mail to the **Harlequin® Reader Service:**
IN U.S.A.: P.O. Box 1867, Buffalo, NY 14240-1867
IN CANADA: P.O. Box 609, Fort Erie, Ontario L2A 5X3

Want to try two free books from another line?
Call 1-800-873-8635 or visit www.ReaderService.com.

* Terms and prices subject to change without notice. Prices do not include applicable taxes. Sales tax applicable in N.Y. Canadian residents will be charged applicable taxes. Offer not valid in Quebec. This offer is limited to one order per household. Not valid for current subscribers to Harlequin American Romance books. All orders subject to credit approval. Credit or debit balances in a customer's account(s) may be offset by any other outstanding balance owed by or to the customer. Please allow 4 to 6 weeks for delivery. Offer available while quantities last.

Your Privacy—The Harlequin® Reader Service is committed to protecting your privacy. Our Privacy Policy is available online at www.ReaderService.com or upon request from the Harlequin Reader Service.

We make a portion of our mailing list available to reputable third parties that offer products we believe may interest you. If you prefer that we not exchange your name with third parties, or if you wish to clarify or modify your communication preferences, please visit us at www.ReaderService.com/consumerschoice or write to us at Harlequin Reader Service Preference Service, P.O. Box 9062, Buffalo, NY 14269. Include your complete name and address.

HAR13R

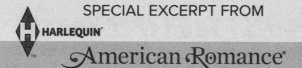
*Looking for more exciting all-American romances like the
one you just read? Read on for an excerpt from
THE COWBOY'S DESTINY by Marin Thomas*

Destiny Saunders marched down the aisle and poked her
head out the door.

Blast you, Daryl.

Even though they'd known each other only six months,
she hadn't expected him to leave her high and dry. She rubbed
her belly. At barely two months pregnant it would be several
weeks before she showed.

She left the chapel, closing the doors behind her. After
stowing her purse and phone, she slid on her mirrored
sunglasses and straddled the seat of her motorcycle, revving
the engine to life. Then she tore out of the parking lot, tires
spewing gravel.

She'd driven only two miles when she spotted a pickup
parked on the shoulder of the road.

A movement caught her attention, and she zeroed in on the
driver's-side window, out of which stuck a pair of cowboy
boots. She approached the vehicle cautiously and peered
through the open window, finding a cowboy sprawled inside,
his hat covering his face.

She slapped her hand against the bottom of one boot
then jumped when the man bolted into an upright position,
knocking his forehead against the rearview mirror.

"Need a lift?"

He glanced at her outfit. "Where's the groom?"

"If I knew that, I wouldn't be talking to you right now."

He shoved his hand out the window. "Buck Cash."

"Destiny Saunders. Where are you headed?"

"Up to Flagstaff for a rodeo this weekend," he replied as he got out of the vehicle.

"What's wrong with your truck?"

"Puncture in one of the hoses."

He peered over her shoulder and she caught a whiff of his cologne. A quiver that had nothing to do with morning sickness spread through her stomach.

"Guess you're going to miss your rodeo," she said.

"There's always another one." He eyed the bike. "This your motorcycle?"

"You think I ditched my fiancé at the altar and then took off on his bike?"

"Kind of looks that way." He kept a straight face but his eyes sparkled.

"Looks can be deceiving. Hop on."

Look for THE COWBOY'S DESTINY
by Marin Thomas in
May 2014 wherever books and ebooks are sold

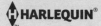
American Romance®

The Secrets Of Horseshoe, Texas

Angie Wiznowski has made mistakes—the biggest is the
secret she's kept from Hardison Hollister for ten years.
The man she loved has the right to know what happened
following that hot Texas night long ago. And it could
cost Angie the most precious thing in her life.

Hardy has no inkling he's a father…until an accident
leaves a young girl injured and the Texas district attorney
with an unexpected addition to his family. Blindsided
by shock and hurt, Hardy can't forgive Angie for her
deception. But as he gets to know his child, old and new
feelings for Angie surface. While scandal could derail
Hardy's political future—is that future meaningless
without Angie and their daughter?

Look for
One Night In Texas
by LINDA WARREN
from Harlequin® American Romance®

Available May 2014
wherever books and ebooks are sold.

www.Harlequin.com

HAR75518